ELIZA BING
IS (NOT)
A BIG, FAT
QUITTER

ELIZA BING IS (NOT) A BIG, FAT QUITTER

Carmella Van Vleet

Holiday House / New York

Library of Congress Cataloging-in-Publication Data

Van Vleet, Carmella.
Eliza Bing is (not) a big, fat quitter / by Carmella Van Vleet. — First edition.
pages cm
Summary: After learning she cannot take a cake decorating class with her best
friend, partly because her parents consider her a quitter, eleven-year-old Eliza tries to
prove herself by sticking with a taekwondo class all summer.
ISBN 978-0-8234-2944-8 (hardcover)
[1. Tae kwon do—Fiction.   2. Martial arts—Fiction.   3. Determination
(Personality trait)—Fiction.   4. Family life—Fiction.   5. Attention-deficit
hyperactivity disorder—Fiction.]   I. Title.
PZ7.V378Eli 2014
[Fic]—dc23
2013015279

For Abbey—my favorite girl in the whole world

ACKNOWLEDGMENTS

Many thanks to my editor, Julie Amper, and all the talented, kind, and dedicated people at Holiday House, including Sally Morgridge, who championed Eliza from the beginning. And to Sylvie Frank, who introduced me to the fold.

I'd also like to deliver a crate of dark chocolate to my agent, Marie Lamba, who turned up at precisely (and I do mean *precisely*) the right moment! Thank you for choosing me to be your first; I'm honored.

To my critique group, aka the MiGs, Kate Fall, Christina Farley, Susan Laidlaw, Andrea Mack, and Debbie Ridpath Ohi: You guys are amazing writers and even better friends. And I'd be remiss if I didn't also mention the tiara-wearing Diane Bailey, who helped turn a ragtag manuscript into something worthy of the ball.

Thank you to Rebecca Mette for crying in the right places. (It could have been the pregnancy hormones. But I'll take it!) And to Stephen Mette, who once told me, "Don't be nervous, be awesome." It's good advice even when you're *not* staring down a pine board that needs breaking.

Thank you Casey Lee for generously and patiently helping me with my Korean.

Thanks also to Tony Boles for being an enthusiastic resource of all things taekwondo, and to my dojang family. It takes courage to step on any martial-art mat, and I'm inspired by all of you who show up and work hard every week. I'd like to especially thank the women black belts I've trained with over the years: Amy, Brenda, Elizabeth, Rebecca, Sarah, and Stacy. I want to be like you when I grow up.

And, of course, my never-ending gratitude goes to Jim, Matt, Sam, and Abbey. You are my sun moon stars rain.

This book contains numerous Korean words. There is a list of these words, their pronunciations, and their definitions at the end of the book to help you as you read.

Translating the Korean language into English is not easy. Like all languages, dialects cause pronunciations to vary from area to area. In addition, each martial arts school may use slightly different terms. I have done my best to use the spelling and pronunciation that the World Taekwondo Federation uses. I have also consulted people who speak Korean. If I've missed the mark on occasion, I apologize. Any errors are mine.

On a final note, one of the characters in this book is testing for her green belt. It should be pointed out that ranking systems vary by school. In other words, a green belt at one school may be a different color or level somewhere else. The ranking system I use here is a fairly traditional one. It is also the one we use at my taekwondo school, and therefore the one I'm most familiar with.

PB AND J

I was peanut butter, and Tony was jelly. That's what our teacher called us after we designed The Tasty Pastry for our fifth-grade social-studies project. Which, FYI, we got a big, fat A on.

"This is so cooool," I said as I wrapped an apron around myself. It was day three of summer, and Dad had dropped me off at the bakery Tony's family owned so I could hang out.

Tony smiled and raised his eyebrow. When Tony first showed up at school, everyone thought that was cool and tried to copy him. I even taped my eyebrow up so it could get used to being in that position. All I managed to do was yank out a bunch of hair when I pulled the tape off.

"The bakery is busy," I noticed out loud.

"Yepperoni!" Tony said, breaking out an Italian accent.

I laughed so hard I got the attention of a nearby cake decorator. She frowned.

Tony ignored her. That was another thing I liked about Tony. Actually, there were lots of things I liked about him. But my favorite was that he never called me names like the other kids. Things like Dizzy Lizzy (which didn't even make sense because my name is *Eliza*, not Lizzy) and Lame Brain (which didn't even rhyme). And when he found out why I went down to the nurse's office each day after second recess, all he did was shrug.

Tony picked up the piping bags on the counter and handed me one. "Here you go."

"Thanks," I said, remembering to use my inside voice that time.

We were supposed to squirt chocolate cream inside cupcakes. That's what Tony had been working on before I came. Tony's mom seemed surprised when I showed up. But on the last day of school, Tony said I could stop by his bakery if I wanted. Any time.

I couldn't believe I was there. I mean, I'd visited once before when Tony and I were doing our project. But this was different. I was really working in a shop! There were pretty, sugary-smelling cakes, cookies, and pastries everywhere. And real, live bakers with flour on their clothes. It was just like the *Sweet Caroline Cakes* TV show.

"It's easy once you get the hang of it," Tony said, showing me how to fill the cupcakes.

We worked for an hour. Tony's whole batch was perfect. I made about a dozen good ones. I kept squeezing the bag of cream too hard, which caused the cupcakes to explode. I had to say "Oops, sorry. Oops, sorry," like a billion times. It was a bona fide cake-tastrophe.

"Clean up in aisle one," Tony said after surveying the damage.

I started giggling and couldn't stop. The grouchy cake decorator was frowning again. Tony's dad came over and told us to take a break and get some cookies from the front case.

"Hey. I've been thinking about our shop's slogan," I said as Tony and I ate our snack at the little table in front of the bakery. He didn't say anything so I kept talking.

"This one is really good. What about 'Sweets for my peeps? Get it? Peeps. Like people?"

"Oh right. Our shop," he said.

I laughed.

Holy cheese and crackers! How could Tony forget The Tasty Pastry? It wasn't just a school project. We were really going to do it someday. He was going to be a world-famous pastry chef. And since I had watched every episode of *Sweet Caroline Cakes* at least three times (including the one where she won the Ohio Cake-Off), Tony said I could be in charge of cakes while he made everything else.

At least that was the plan.

THE BIG FAT NO

My dad says some ideas are like Venus flytraps and that lots of times, I'm the bug. I don't know if it's true or not; but when the summer brochure for the community center came in the mail, I circled Cakes with Caroline with a red marker. Then I dog-eared the page and left the brochure open on the counter for Mom.

Sweet Caroline was the nicest person on TV. She always treated clients like old friends and didn't yell at her employees. She ended every episode by looking at the camera and saying, "Be sweet to those you meet."

Tony was already signed up for the class, which was being held in a room filled with kitchenettes where you could work with real ovens and wear real chef hats. Even though cakes weren't his specialty, he still thought it was important to know how to do them. And the bakers at his parents' shop didn't have the time to teach him.

After I got home from hanging out with Tony at the bakery, I went into the kitchen to grab a hot dog from the fridge and ask Mom if she'd registered me yet.

When she saw me, Mom stopped rinsing dishes and sat down at the kitchen table.

"Come have a seat," she said.

Being asked to sit down is never a good sign.

I broke off an end of the cold hot dog and dangled it above Bear. She wagged her stumpy poodle tail so hard her whole backside shook, but then she remembered her manners and sat down. I gave the piece to Bear and then took my own bite.

"Eliza. Honey," Mom said. (*Honey* isn't a good sign, either.) "Dad and I talked it over, and we decided it wasn't a good idea for you to take the cake-decorating class."

I forgot the swallow-first-then-talk rule and choked a little. "Why not?" I asked between coughs.

Mom frowned. "Well," she said, "the class is twice as expensive as all the other classes. Plus you have to buy a book and extra materials. At the moment, we just can't afford it. Not with Dad changing career directions."

Changing career directions was code for "losing his job and going back to college." It meant I heard, "We can't afford it," as often as I heard Mom say, "I can't today. I have to work."

"But Mom . . ."

"Isn't there another class you'd like to take instead?" She gave me a hopeful smile.

I crossed my arms and gave *her* my best stink eye. "No!"

NO J

I was too mad to eat so I gave Bear the rest of the hot dog. Then I grabbed the phone, locked myself in the bathroom, and called Tony.

"Oh man," he said when I told him the bad news. "That sucks raw eggs."

"I know! It's so unfair."

"Maybe you could pay for the extra stuff," Tony suggested. "Do you have any money?"

Even though I was on the phone, I shook my head. "I only have ten dollars."

"That's not enough," Tony said.

"Nope."

I thought he might offer to share the money he got from helping at his family's bakery, but he didn't.

Neither of us said anything for a minute. I tugged on

my lucky rubber band, the one I wore around my ankle. It snapped in half.

"So I guess I'll let you know how the class goes," Tony finally said.

Whoomph! That took all the air out of my chest.

"You're still gonna take it?" I asked. "Without me?"

"Duh," Tony said.

When I didn't say anything, Tony went on in a nicer voice. "If I'm gonna be a pastry chef, I gotta get started."

"I think you're being selfish," I told him.

"Well, I think *you're* being selfish. Being a pastry chef is my thing."

"Mine too!" I said. "Well, cake decorating anyway."

"Since when?"

I could feel the anger rolling around my insides. Why didn't he think I was serious? I talked about Sweet Caroline's cake show all the time. He said that's why he picked me to be his partner on the create-your-own-business project. He told me he could tell I was going be a great cake decorator someday.

I opened my mouth to take a deep breath, but instead of air coming in, something else popped out. "Jerk."

Tony hung up.

PB without J.

That's what I was.

NOT THE MARTIAL-ARTS TYPE

Heads up: I'm switching channels. I do that sometimes.

On Wednesday afternoon, I went to the community center with Dad and Sam, my older dork brother. Mom had to work an extra shift at the hospital. (Big surprise.)

When I said I wanted to stay home alone, Mom told me to look in the mirror and introduce myself to the girl there, ha-ha. At least she didn't point to the water spot on the kitchen ceiling or the strawberry-syrup stain on the carpet or the picture of me with uneven bangs like she sometimes did. For the record, I did those things before I was diagnosed. *And* when I was much younger.

"I'm eleven," I reminded Mom.

"Yeah. I know," she said, taking her nurse's scrubs out of the dryer. "I was there when you were born."

I didn't think her joke was funny. And I still had to ride along to the community center and sit bored out of my mind at a table in the hallway while Sam took a taekwondo class and Dad cut out leaves from construction paper. By the way, my dad's not a weirdo who likes to cut paper leaves for fun. He's just a guy who got laid off from his desk job and went back to college to become a teacher. Which, if you think about it, is also kind of a desk job. The leaves were for one of his classes. They were doing a unit on making bulletin boards.

When taekwondo class was over, Sam had a scowl on his face. That wasn't unusual. Mom liked to joke that all fifteen-year-old boys take a secret oath to scowl a minimum of five hours a day.

"I'm done," he said.

"Okay," Dad said, standing up. "Just let me and Eliza pack up our stuff."

"No," Sam said. "I mean, I don't want to go back."

Dad narrowed his eyes.

"I'm not the martial-arts type," Sam said.

"You can't decide that after one class," Dad told him.

"Sure I can," Sam insisted.

"So you're going to waste all your hard-earned money?" Dad asked.

That seemed strange to me, too. Sam had used his lawn-mowing money to pay for half of the class fee. He'd been all gung ho ever since he found out one of the other drummers in the marching band took jujitsu or something like that.

"It's my money to blow," Sam said. "Besides, you don't want me to break a finger, do you? I can't hold sticks if I'm wearing a cast."

"I'm sure it's perfectly safe," Dad said.

"It's just a bunch of babies," Sam said, sweeping his hand in the direction of the kids in white uniforms. "I'm the oldest one."

Just then a pretty teenage girl walked by. Sam blushed.

"What about her?" Dad said, pointing. "She looks around sixteen."

The girl noticed we were talking about her and gave us a shy smile.

Sam waited until she was out of earshot. "Dad. She's a black belt."

"So?"

"So I'm *not*," Sam said.

Dad considered this a moment. "You're really gonna let your pride get in the way?"

"I don't want to come back next week," Sam said, tilting his chin. That was Sam's way of saying he'd made up his mind.

"Fine." That was Dad's way of saying, "Do whatever you want."

Great, I thought. I'm dying to take a class but can't. And Sam *gets* to take a class and then quits?

In the history of all unfair things in the world, this had to be in the top ten.

THE PART WHERE I FOUND OUT THE TRUTH

If you hide on the first step above the landing, you can hear what people are saying in our kitchen. This is how I discovered why Mom and Dad *really* said no to the cake class.

"I just don't think it's such a good idea," Mom said.

"I know," Dad said. "But I can't help but feel guilty. It's my fault money is tight."

Mom started banging some pots around. She had to start dinner because Dad forgot to write a Sticky Note, reminding himself to do it. Sticky Notes were Dad's thing. He used so many that Mom bought them in bulk at Save Club.

"Should we have spaghetti or spaghetti?" Mom asked.

Dad laughed and told her spaghetti sounded good. (My parents are so weird.) There were more cooking noises. Pots and spoons banging. Water running. The refrigerator being opened and closed. I listened hard.

"What's really going on?" Dad asked. His voice had turned serious again.

There was a pause; then Mom spoke. "I'm worried it'll be just another thing she quits after a couple of weeks."

I nearly toppled off the step. Did I hear that right?

Mom went on, "I think the only reason she wants to is because the woman from the cable show is teaching it."

"What's wrong with that? It's her favorite show," Dad said.

"Nothing," Mom said. "Except I'd bet my last cup of coffee that the novelty will wear off after a few weeks."

"Yeah, but who knows? Maybe she won't quit *this* time," Dad said.

I missed the rest of the conversation because Sam came out of his bedroom and caught me on the stairs.

"Eavesdrop much?" he asked.

I glared at him, and he shrugged. "Just saying," he said.

"Be a pain much?" I asked. "Just saying."

Sam grinned; but instead of getting into it with him, I went to my room and threw myself down on the bed to think.

QUITTER

I'm worried it'll be just another thing she quits.
Who knows? Maybe she won't quit this time.

What Mom and Dad said played over and over in my head.

I said it out loud. "Quit. Quit. Quit." It sounded weird. Like a funny bird call.

"Quitter."

It sounded hard. Like a kick. Not like a bird at all.

I couldn't believe it.

Mom and Dad said I was a quitter.

It made my heart hurt.

I thought about all the things I'd tried. Junior Scouts had too many people. Gymnastics had too much waiting. Tap had too many blisters. And piano had too many rules. ("Keep your wrists high and fingers soft," Miss Logan always told me. And, "You must practice twenty minutes every day." Bah!) I wasn't a quitter. I just got bored fast. But that's the way my brain works. Fast. Before I figured out how to slow my thoughts down, they were like those go-carts at the arcade that buzz round and round the track so crazy that they miss the guy with the checkered flag, pointing to the exit ramp.

As hard as I tried not to, I thought of something else, too.

I thought about one night, a few weeks after Dad lost his job. By then he'd decided to go back to college. I couldn't turn my brain off, so I went downstairs to get some water and to warm my blanket in the dryer.

"What are you doing up so late?" Mom asked me. "Couldn't sleep?"

I nodded and plopped down on the couch in between her and Dad.

Dad had his laptop perched on the armrest. "Whatcha working on?" I asked.

"My college-application essay."

I laid my head down on Mom's lap and let her stroke my hair while I watched the late-night talk show on TV.

I don't know how long I laid there before my eyelids got heavy. I was only half awake when Mom nudged me.

Then I heard her tell my dad, "You need to go to bed, too. You're exhausted."

"Can't," he said. "You know the saying, 'Losers quit when they're tired. Winners quit when they've won.'"

Mom chuckled. Then she helped me upstairs and tucked me in.

Losers quit. Dad said so. And Mom had laughed.

Did that mean they thought *I* was a loser?

I stayed in my room until Mom called me downstairs and asked me to clear the table for dinner.

The whole time I did this, I tried not to look at Mom and Dad. But they weren't even paying attention to the fact that I wasn't speaking to them.

And when it came time to eat, I kept my eyes on my plate. We had spaghetti, no meat, store-brand sauce, and garlic bread made out of old hamburger buns. *Again.* But that wasn't the reason I wasn't eating.

It's hard to swallow when there's a big lump in your throat.

THE PART WHERE I WAS HIT BY LIGHTNING

The next day, Mom had the day off. She went grocery shopping early. Sometimes I went with her, but I was still upset about being called a quitter and didn't go.

I was sitting in the living room, reading, when I heard the garage door rumble open. Dad walked through on his way to help unload.

"Eliza," he said, "please make space for the groceries."

I gathered up some old mail and moved it onto the kitchen island, which Dad called the Holding Pen and Mom called the Bermuda Triangle. As I laid the stuff down, I noticed the community-center summer brochure.

Maybe I'll tear it into a million pieces, I thought. Or maybe I'll just crumple it or shove it in the trash and then dump old scrambled eggs on top of it.

But instead of doing any of these things, I opened the brochure to the Cakes with Caroline page. I guess I just wanted to torture myself one last time by reading the class description:

Bring those aprons and spatulas and join "Sweet" Caroline McKinny from the hit television show Sweet Caroline Cakes *in this basic cake class! We'll learn how* to create scrumptious cakes from scratch and how to decorate them.

I couldn't go on reading. It made me too sad.

But here's the thing. My eyes jumped to the dates and times and room number of the class and that's when I noticed something way at the bottom, in parentheses:

This class will be held again in the fall.

There was another class!

Standing there in the kitchen, I got hit with a lightning-bolt idea.

It was the perfect way to get into the fall cake class with Sweet Caroline *and* to prove to Mom and Dad I wasn't a quitter.

I STRIKE A DEAL

That night I found Mom and Dad sitting on the deck in Adirondack Chairs.

"Hey kiddo," Dad said, popping open a soda. "Nice night, huh?"

"Yep," I agreed. And it really was. It was just getting dark and a few fireflies blinked Morse code. *Catch-me. Catch-me.*

I settled on the bench across from them and began digging at a splinter in my big toe.

Mom started to get out of her chair.

"I got it," I told her. "It's just a little one."

Mom didn't move. "Those are the worst kind. Are you sure you don't need help?"

I hated the way she treated me like a baby sometimes. "I said I got it," I told her.

Mom lowered herself back down. "Make sure you wash your hands and put some antibacterial cream on that after you get it out," she said. "You wouldn't believe how many nasty infections we see at the hospital."

Here was my opening, the perfect spot to put my plan in motion.

"What's the weirdest case you saw today?" I asked Mom.

"Well, we had this one toddler," Mom said. She paused then chuckled. "The poor little guy got his hand stuck inside the gum-ball machine at a grocery store. The EMTs couldn't get his hand out, so they just loaded up the boy and the gum machine and transported them together!"

"That sounds like something out of a bad movie," Dad said.

"Or a really good one," I said.

Mom and Dad laughed.

Then I went for it. "I bet you've seen it all, huh, Mom?"

"Just about," Mom agreed.

"I bet you've never seen a cake-decorating injury, though," I said.

Mom didn't lose her grin, but her eyes narrowed a bit. "Are you still on that kick?"

"It's not a kick," I told her. "I really want to take the class."

Dad spoke up. "Eliza. I'm sorry. We just can't afford it."

Mom jumped in on the act. "You know we had to use savings to pay for Dad's tuition and—"

"I heard you," I blurted out. "When you were in the kitchen last night. You guys said it was because you thought I just wanted to meet Sweet Caroline and that I'd quit like always."

Mom and Dad looked at each other.

Mom sighed and then turned toward me. "I'm sorry you overheard that. And no one said, 'Like always,' " she said gently. "But you have to admit, your track record isn't great."

"What if I proved I wasn't a quitter?"

"We don't think you're a quitter," Mom said, "It's just—"

Dad interrupted. "Wait. How would you do that?"

Sweet taffy! I had him!

"There's another class in the fall. What if I take Sam's place in the taekwondo class all summer? And don't quit. Then will you let me take the next session?"

Mom studied me a moment. "I don't know. . . ."

"But the class is already paid for," I reminded her. "It wouldn't cost you a thing! In fact, it'd be like I was *saving* you money." (That last part I came up with at the spur of the moment.)

"Do you really think you'd want to do that?" Dad asked.

I shrugged. "Sure. It sounds kind of fun."

Mom threw up her hands in defeat. "Okay," she said. "Deal."

I blinked a few times. Mom *never* gives a green light that quickly.

I jumped up and ran inside before she could change her mind. "Deal!" I called over my shoulder.

This was great. All I had to do was stick out taekwondo for the summer. How hard could it be? Kick, punch, and yell hi-ya! every once in a while? Things could go back to the way they were supposed to be.

And Mom and Dad wouldn't think I was a quitter.

STUPID

After I got back inside, I grabbed the phone and dialed Tony's number.

"I'm sorry I called you a jerk," I told him.

"It's all right," Tony said. "Sorry I hung up on you."

"Guess what. I think I might be able to take the fall class." I told him my plan and then asked, "Why don't you wait? That way we can take it together."

"Nah," he said. "I wanna take it over the summer."

Sometimes my mouth works faster than my brain. What happened next was one of those times.

"You're stupid!" I said.

And for the second time that week, Tony hung up on me.

WAR, BUT NOT THE BAD KIND

On Friday I found Mom straightening up the kitchen. When she saw me, she held out a pair of scissors.

"Eliza, honey. Can you please put these away?"

"Sure." I told her.

I pulled open the junk drawer. There was a deck of cards near the front.

"Hey, Mom. How about a game of War?"

Mom finished wiping some crumbs off the table and grinned. "Okay! Why not?"

It'd been a long time since Mom and I had played War. We used to do it all the time before she had to go back to work. It was kind of our thing, and we'd always end up laughing and talking. Mom called it our "kitchen sink" time cause we discussed everything but the kitchen sink.

Mom shuffled and dealt. Right away I lost a king when we had a war of threes and she pulled an ace.

"So," Mom said after a couple of rounds. "Are you looking forward to taekwondo tomorrow?"

I considered her question. "Yeah. I guess," I told her. "I liked *The Karate Kid*."

Mom laughed. "Things are never like they are in the movies!"

I figured she was probably right, but it still kind of annoyed me that she laughed.

After I won back my king and took the rest of the cards, Mom suggested we make popcorn.

I wrinkled my nose.

"Since when do you not like popcorn?" Mom asked.

It wasn't that I didn't like popcorn. But for the last few months, we'd given up the pop-in-the-bag microwave kind and had been making it in brown paper bags instead. Which still, technically, was microwave popcorn since we put it in the microwave to cook. But it wasn't the same. It was too plain. And weird: No other families I knew made popcorn that way. Mom said it was cheaper, though.

"I think we're out of paper bags," I said. (It *could've* been true.)

"Then I'll show you how to make it the old-fashioned way," Mom said. "I need the popcorn and vegetable oil."

It turned out that the old-fashioned way meant putting oil and popcorn in a lidded pot and shaking it over a lit hot-stove burner.

I was skeptical, but sure enough a few minutes into shaking the pot, I heard the *ping ping ping* of kernels popping. It smelled heavenly! After Mom dumped the fluffy white popcorn into a bowl, she melted some margarine in the hot pan.

"This is how me and my friends used to make popcorn when we had sleepovers," Mom said.

I tried to imagine what it was like to have a sleepover.

I had a few friends. Or at least people who were nice to me. But I didn't have any sleepover friends. There was this one girl when I was in third grade. Naomi. She was in my Jitter Lunch Bunch. She had ADHD, too. The rest of the kids called us the Double Trouble Twins to our faces, but we didn't care. She gave me half of a best-friends heart necklace. But Naomi's family moved the following the year, and that was that. *Adios muchachos.*

After Tony and I did our Tasty Pastry project, people started talking to me more. Some of the girls even asked me to sit with them at lunch. But I had no idea what was going to happen once I started middle school.

What if no one liked me? A bigger school could just mean more people who thought I was weird. The teachers could be mean or not give me more time for tests or not let me take a break when I needed to get up and walk around. And the middle school was huge. We had a field trip there once to see a play. It was two stories and had tons of rooms.

I swallowed hard. "Um," I said, "so do you think I'll be invited to sleepovers next year?" I tried to sound like it was no big deal if I was or wasn't.

Mom smiled. "Sure! And I'll make my famous stove-top popcorn," she said, waving the bowl of warm, buttery popcorn under my nose.

"I don't know. . . ."

"You'll see," Mom said, sounding like a chirpy mother on one of those Hallmark Channel shows where everything works out. "Middle school will be great."

I tried to smile back.

Mom said movies weren't like real life. I wondered if she knew real life wasn't like the movies, either.

MY FIRST TAEKWONDO CLASS, OR WHEN I FOUND OUT MASTER KIM HAD NINJA POWERS

It was Saturday, and I was standing in the back of the room, wiggling my toes and wondering if I should switch to orange nail polish since pink is so pink. Someone walked over and parked his feet in front of mine. I knew the feet were a man's because the toes were long and kind of hairy.

I looked up.

"You must be my new student," the man said. "Welcome. I am Master Kim." He put out his hand.

Master Kim was around my dad's age. He wasn't short or super tall; but his shoulders were wide, and he had big hands that looked like they could crush a brick. His eyes were dark, and he had a long, black ponytail. His uniform was white and crisp. But his belt was frayed and more gray than black. I wondered why he didn't just get a new one.

I opened my mouth to reply, but then I noticed a boy with an orange belt standing several feet behind Master Kim. He was pointing at Master Kim and bowing. I ignored it because of the try-to-focus speech Dad had given me on the ride over.

I looked Master Kim in the eye. This is a trick Mom taught me to do when I needed to give someone my full attention.

"Nice to meet you. I'm Eliza Bing," I said, shaking his hand. (In my head, I added, *Bing. Like the cherry.*)

"And you, as well, Eliza," Master Kim said. "Please ask your father to find me after class so we can arrange to get you a *dobok* and a belt."

I figured *dobok* meant "uniform." But I didn't know how Master Kim knew my dad was the person who brought me. I nodded anyway. It's the polite thing to do, after all.

Master Kim leaned in closer. "By the way," he said, "what the young man behind me is trying to tell you is that it is proper martial-arts etiquette to bow whenever you greet a black belt."

My brain screeched to a halt.

How did Master Kim know what the boy behind him was doing? Did taekwondo masters have some kind of super-ninja power?

"A good martial artist is always aware of his or her environment," Master Kim said.

Speechless, I nodded like a bobble-head. Master Kim turned and strode to the front of the class. He seemed to fill up the whole room.

"*Jong yul!*" he called. "Class, line up!"

There were about twenty students, and they began to move themselves around like they were setting up an invisible chessboard. I don't know if the class was really "ages seven to seventeen" like the brochure said, but Sam was right. It was mostly kids my age or younger. Some of the students had orange or yellow or gold belts tied around their waists. They lined up in the front of the class. Almost everyone else had on white belts. They stood in the back rows. There were two teenagers wearing black belts. They stood behind everyone else. One of them, the girl, smiled at me and pointed to an open spot on the carpet.

I hurried to where she was motioning and stood at attention, proud I'd done it so quickly. It wasn't until I was there for a few seconds that I remembered the rule about bowing to black belts.

THINGS THAT WERE HARD

1. Remembering to say, "Yes sir," and bow. And there's a *lot* of bowing.
2. Remembering to *kihap* (that means "yell") when you kick or punch.
3. Counting to ten in Korean. (I tried to follow along in my head but got confused around number five, and then the rest of the class left me behind.)
4. Having the instructor stand and watch your every move and never smile.

AND THE OTHER THING

During class Master Kim had us form two lines. I got in the line with the black-belt helper. She bowed to Master Kim, and he bowed back and handed her a black rectangular pad. Then he picked up his own pad and said, "We're going to work on our board breaks."

The boy behind me gave a little moan. When I looked

over my shoulder, he whispered, "I got jump front kick. It's *hard*."

I nodded in sympathy. I didn't know what a jump front kick was. But the boy had a patch on his *dobok* sleeve that said BEST KICKING. If *he* thought it was hard, I was in trouble.

Each person took a turn kicking the pad and then ran to the back of the line. When it was my turn, I just stood there, waiting.

"Oh!" the black belt said. "That's right. You're new. The white belt break is push kick."

She motioned to the boy behind me. "Please demonstrate, Mark." I was supposed to stand in fighting stance, with my fists up, and then move my back leg up and pull my knee as tight as I could to my body.

"Now fire out your leg," the black belt said. "And hit the target with the ball of your foot."

"Make sure you don't point your toes," Mark said. "Or you might break one."

Great. Broken toes were not fun. I knew that from experience. When I was nine, I jumped off the couch, broke my big toe, and had to wear a stupid-looking boot-slipper thing for a month.

I tried to do what Mark had done, but when my foot shot out, it barely hit the pad.

"Not bad," the black belt said with a smile. But her "not bad" didn't sound all that good.

I went to the back of the line. I got to practice a few

more times. Each time something went wrong. My kick was too wide. Or too short. I forgot to *kihap*.

At one point, Master Kim handed his kicking pad over to another black belt and came over to watch me.

"You're not following through," he said. "Don't kick at it. Kick past it."

"Yes sir," I said.

But I had no idea what he meant. How could you kick something if you were aiming past it?

Master Kim sounded like Yoda. And not in a good way.

THERE'S GONNA BE A TEST?!

At the end of class, Master Kim had an announcement. "*Ahnjoe*. Sit down," he told us.

I sat cross-legged and put my hands on my knees like everyone else. Well, everyone except Master Kim. He sat down like he was kneeling but with his behind resting on his lower legs and heels. His hands were laced together in an O in his lap. How could he sit like that? It didn't look comfortable. Then again, I liked to hang my head off the end of the couch and let the blood rush to my head, which Mom said looked uncomfortable.

My stomach growled. I wondered what was for dinner and if Mom's shift was going to be over early enough for her to eat with us. Maybe I'd get the cards out, and we could have a War rematch afterward. Or maybe I'd ask her to make popcorn and try to talk to her again about middle school.

". . . belt test will be August fifteenth," Master Kim was saying. "In the coming weeks, you'll be learning all your requirements, including your *poomsae*, or form."

Hold the phone. . . . Did he just say *test*?

I turned to my neighbor and whispered, "Did he just say—"

But my neighbor gave me look that said, "Be quiet." So I looked at Master Kim and scrambled my brain to the right channel instead.

"If you are a new student," Master Kim said, "please see me after class so I can give you a student handbook. Your handbook is your responsibility, not your parents'. Put it in a safe place and do not lose it. You will need it to study."

I had to study? Over the *summer*?

I bet Cakes with Caroline didn't have studying.

Master Kim called, "*Yursit!*"

The rest of the white belts kind of looked around, but the kids with colored belts got up. I figured *yursit* meant "stand up," so I stood up, too.

The boy who bowed us into class was in charge again. "Class, *charyut*." He stood straight with his fists at his side. Then he said, "*Kyoonyae,*" and bowed. Everyone followed his lead, and a few people said some word I didn't understand.

Master Kim bowed. "*Hae sahn!* Class dismissed."

Afterward the white belts lined up by Master Kim. Each time he handed someone a folder, he bowed. When it was my turn, I bowed, too. "Thank you."

"*Kamsahhamida,*" he said. "That's how you say thank you in Korean. And by the way, *cheonman-eyo.* You're welcome."

Sheesh.

IN CASE YOU'RE WONDERING

Mom didn't make it home until after Dad put away the leftovers and started the dishwasher. There was no War or old-fashioned popcorn that night. Just Mom's soft snoring coming from the couch.

STICKY NOTE TO SELF: WEAR WHITE UNDERWEAR ON WEDNESDAYS AND SATURDAYS

On Wednesday I had my second taekwondo class. For once I was ready to go someplace on time. And with the help of a few green lights, Dad and I even got to the community center ten minutes early. Master Kim was in the hallway.

"Eliza," he called, motioning me and Dad over.

"Yes?"

"Yes *sir*," Dad prompted, nodding at Master Kim.

"Yes sir," I said.

Master Kim smiled and bowed. "Here is your *dobok*. You can change in the restroom. When you are ready, come find me, and I will put on your belt."

I returned the bow and took the plastic bag with the uniform.

The bathroom stall was kind of small, and it took some Houdinilike twisting to get changed as quickly as I could. At the end of the first class, Mark had told me you do push-ups if you were late, and I did *not* want to find out if he was just trying to scare me.

The bathroom tile was cold from the air-conditioning. I put my shorts and flip-flops in the plastic bag. (I kept my T-shirt on since the *dobok* had a deep V collar. The last thing I wanted to do was flash my sports bra, thank you very much.) On the way out of the restroom, I pulled up the long top and checked out my backside in the mirror. I wanted to make sure you couldn't see my pink underwear through the white pants. I found that when I was standing straight, I was okay. But if I leaned over, even just a little, the pink showed through. I groaned.

"Looks good," Dad said when he saw me.

I glanced down. The sleeves and pant legs went way past my fingertips and toes. "It's too big."

"Not as big as Sam's was," Dad said.

Boy, that was the truth. Sam's *dobok* top hung down to my knees. There was no way I could use it.

"Don't worry," Dad went on. "It'll shrink in the wash. If not, Mom can hem it. Here. Let's roll up it up in the meantime." Dad knelt in front of me like I was a little kid and began rolling up the pant legs. I would have protested, but I didn't feel like bending over and showing off my colorful underwear to the people behind me. In fact, I didn't feel like moving at all. The *dobok* was so stiff. It was like wearing clothes made out of paper, and I hated anything that was even remotely uncomfortable. Even worse? It made a *scritch-scritch* noise when I walked.

"That's the best we can do for now," Dad said, straightening up. "Besides, it was lucky for us Master Kim had this extra one you could use."

I almost asked why he and Mom were willing to buy Sam a *dobok* for his class but not decorator tips and a book for mine. And I really wanted to point out that Sam had ended up being the quitter, not me. But I figured it wasn't the time or place. Mom is always reminding me about needing to find the right time and place to share what's on my mind.

I held out my arms so Dad could roll the sleeves up, too.

"The pants hang too low," I said.

"Well, just roll down the waistband a couple of times." I could tell Dad was trying to sound all cheerful but getting irritated.

"You'll see," Dad said. "It'll soften up in the wash, too." He winked. "I'll use extra fabric softener."

I'd just finished rolling down the waistband when Master Kim walked over. He was carrying a folded white belt. "This is a *dee*," he said. "Please raise your arms."

Master Kim spread the belt across my stomach and wrapped the belt around my back and then back in front again. He was quick and precise. "It is tradition that a black belt ties on each new belt," he explained. "White represents a new beginning."

Before I knew it, Master Kim pulled in opposite directions, and my belt had a perfect knot. I don't know how he did it, but the two ends hanging down were exactly even. I liked when things were even.

Sweet Caroline liked things even, too. Whenever she messed up a line of piping or cut a piece of fondant crooked, she'd do it over until it was perfect. I remember one show where she remade an entire wedding cake just because the color of the frosting was not exactly right. I would have been mad, but Caroline just looked at the camera, smiled, and said, "Creating something wonderful takes time."

??? !!!

Master Kim started class with meditation. We were supposed to sit cross-legged and rest our hands on our knees, close our eyes, and think about breathing.

Church bells, it was boring! And every time I tried to concentrate on inhaling or exhaling, it was like I completely forgot how to breathe altogether. After about thirty seconds, I gave up and tried to remember how to spell *breathe*. Does it have an e on the end or not?

When Master Kim finally said, "*Yursit!* Stand up!" I jumped.

Thankfully we started moving after that. We did some stretching and then running. I had to keep my head down so I didn't trip over my long pants, which had come unrolled.

"We're going to work on escapes," Master Kim said when we were done running. "Everyone find a partner."

My chest still pounded from the running as I looked around. Most of the kids seemed to know each other. In an instant, the whole room had paired up! I was a lone sock. A single glove. I was trying to come up with a third thing when I heard my name.

"Eliza, please come here," Master Kim said from the other end of the room. For one horrible, horrible second I thought I'd have to be his partner. But it turned out to be even worse.

That's because standing next to Master Kim was none other than Madison Green.

With a big, fake smile on her face.

TIME OUT; REWIND

One day at lunch, I made the mistake of sitting too close to Madison and her friends.

One of the girls, Janet, walked by and squirted juice on the seat next to me. Then she started yelling at me to clean up *my* mess. That got the attention of the lunch monitor. I guess the girls didn't want to get in trouble because Madison stood up and said, "I'll get some napkins." But Janet told her, "No. It's Eliza's mess," and Madison sat back down.

When I was getting the napkins, the girls filled my lunch bag with trash.

But that wasn't even the worst thing. Once we had a sub in social studies who let us spend the hour talking and playing Hangman. The girls were giggling over a note. I asked what was so funny, but they wouldn't tell me. Tony swiped the note, which was written in this big, loopy handwriting. Madison had written that I should be called Every Day Eliza because I wore the same clothes to school every day. She swore she didn't write it, but I knew it was her. And I'd never, ever forget the way she'd dotted her *i*'s with big swirls instead of dots. Most of her friends just put dumb hearts or stars. But I guess Madison just *had* to be different.

Even though Tony crumpled the note and threw it away, word got around. I tried to explain that I like to wear the same worn-in clothes because I want to be comfortable. I can't stand tags or itchy material. But no one paid attention. And pretty soon everyone was calling me Every Day Eliza.

I tried to laugh.

I tried to pretend it didn't bother me.

I begged and begged until I convinced Mom to take me shopping for a few new outfits. But the name still stuck like a rash.

People say you can't judge a book by its cover, but I say when it's shelved in the Mean Girl section you don't have to check it out to know it's gonna stink.

PARTNERS

I stared at Madison.

Where had she come from? I didn't know how I could have missed her before.

"Eliza, you can partner with Madison," Master Kim said, waving a hand her direction. "You two are similar size."

"Yes sir," Madison and I said at the same time.

Master Kim returned to the front of the room.

I looked at Madison's waist. An orange belt. I quickly checked the belt poster hanging on the wall. Great. Orange was three whole ranks above white.

"Hi," Madison said, still smiling.

"Um. Hey," I replied.

"I've been on vacation," she explained as if she'd read my mind. "We just got back yesterday."

I was confused. She actually sounded kind of nice.

"Oh," I said.

I looked down. Only one of Madison's feet had painted toenails. I was going to ask why because I couldn't think of anything else to say. Well, that's not entirely true. But I didn't think saying, "Great. I can't believe I'm stuck with *you*," out loud would be very polite. Plus I don't actually say *everything* that pops into my head.

Fortunately Master Kim began giving instructions on how to escape from a wrist grab. *Unfortunately*, he didn't talk for long.

When it came time to practice with our partners, Madison and I kind of stood there. I didn't really talk to her at school much—even before the lunch-table thing or the note.

Madison glanced in Master Kim's direction. "We should practice," she said.

She thrust out her arm. "Here, you grab me, and I'll show you what to do."

I grabbed her right wrist with my right hand.

"First off, open your fist and spread your fingers as wide as you can," she told me as she demonstrated. "That helps loosen the person's grip. Figure out where their finger and thumb touch—that's their weak point—and yank your hand through that spot quickly."

Madison *kihapped*, "*High-shhh!*", pulled her arm from my grasp, and stepped back so she could be ready to run or fight me if I was really a kidnapper.

She made it look easy. Not that I was about to tell *her* that.

I grabbed Madison's wrist a few more times. She escaped no problem. "Now you try," she commanded.

I went over the steps in my head. Open fist and pull quickly. It took a little muscle, but my arm came free!

"Don't forget to *kihap*," Madison said.

"Oh yeah. Right. I keep forgetting that."

It was a lie. I didn't keep forgetting to yell each time I did something—I just didn't want to. Master Kim said it was important because it helped focus our power and show confidence. But it made me feel like everyone was watching me. And no matter what some of my teachers or the kids at school thought, I didn't like attention all the time.

My second attempt at a wrist escape was a little better. I gave a halfhearted *kihap*, too. Everyone's yell was a little different; mine came out sounding like *huuup*.

I held out my arm a third time. Madison gripped it even tighter than before, but I still managed to get myself free.

I was about to try it again, when Master Kim walked over and stood behind Madison.

"Please demonstrate your technique," he said.

I grabbed Madison's wrist, and she escaped easily, just like before.

"Good," he told her.

Madison beamed and then grabbed my wrist.

I planned what I was going to do: Open hand, pull, *kihap*, get ready to run. It all went smoothly in my head; but when I tried to pull my arm away, Madison's fingers wrapped tighter around my wrist.

Hay bales! She wanted me to fail!

Now *this* was the Madison I knew.

No matter how hard I pulled or how loudly I *kihapped*, I couldn't escape.

After five or six tries, Master Kim stopped me. I was hoping he'd scold Madison for holding on so tightly, but he didn't.

"If you can't escape right away, attack," he said. "A good martial artist adapts."

I'm guessing a good martial artist refrains from punching her partner in the nose, too, I thought.

After Master Kim left, I turned to Madison. "Why did you do that?"

"Do what?" she said, all innocentlike.

"Hold on so tight?"

Madison put a hand on one of her hips. "I wouldn't be doing you any favors by making it easy," she said.

Of course. Why would she suddenly do me any favors?

A LESSON IN
FON-DON'T

The next morning was as gray and soggy as a soaked sock. I had to shove Bear's butt to get her to go through the doggy door to do her business because the thunder made her nervous.

One of Dad's Sticky Notes was on the cabinet: DON'T FORGET LUNCH. But I discovered his brown bag in the fridge when I went to get some juice. The kitchen lights were on, too. (Mom must have left before Dad did.) I turned the lights off. I love when the house feels all dark and cozy. Especially in summer.

I curled up on the couch and put in a DVD of the first

season of *Sweet Caroline Cakes*. After finding out Madison was in my taekwondo class, I needed some cheering up.

After a few shows, I decided to dig out the cake-decorating book I got at the beginning of May, when Tony and I were doing our project. I was thinking about getting Tony a copy for his birthday in August. I figured the two of us would work things out before then. Not that we were going to hang out constantly or anything once we got to sixth grade. He was a guy after all, and I knew it didn't work that way in middle school. But as long as we were friends, maybe things would be okay.

I stretched out on the living-room floor and flipped through the thick spiral book. There was a whole section on wedding cakes and another on birthday cakes, but my favorite section was the one on novelty cakes. I studied each page, trying to figure out how the bakers did it. One cake looked like a giant hamburger with a sesame bun and a side order of fries. Another one was shaped like a toilet! There was even one that looked like a newspaper sitting on grass. That one had a picture and writing you could really read. It said: BUSINESS NEWS OF THE WEEK: DAVE RETIRES.

The book said every great baker should know how to make fondant, so I decided to give it a shot. Fondant was the smooth doughlike frosting Sweet Caroline used all the time. She draped it on her cakes or cut all kinds of designs and ribbons out of it. When we were doing our project, Tony and I had helped one of the decorators at his parents' shop make fondant. Big Frankie threw the ingredients into a mixer that was as tall as my waist. When I accidentally turned the machine on too high, Tony and I got covered in powdered sugar. It was hysterical.

There were two recipes in the frosting chapter. One was for marshmallow fondant ("a quick and easy version," the book said) and the other one was for almond-flavored fondant ("for more experienced decorators"). After watching all those episodes of *Sweet Caroline Cakes*, I figured I fell into the experienced-decorator category.

We had almost all the ingredients: almond extract, light corn syrup, confectioners sugar, and shortening. We even had the unflavored gelatin because Dad made his own jellies and jams for Christmas presents. The only thing we didn't have on the ingredients list was glycerin. I didn't know what it was, but since the recipe called for only one tablespoon of it, I figured it couldn't be that important.

Everything started out fine. I followed the recipe exactly and kneaded and kneaded until my fingers felt like they were about to fall off. But instead of getting a nice ball of soft dough, all I got was a sticky mess. I tried adding a little more confectioners sugar. And then I tried putting shortening on my hands so the fondant wouldn't stick. These things didn't help. Nothing did. It looked like someone melted taffy all over the kitchen counter.

I used my foot to open the cabinet under the sink where we kept the trash can and threw out the whole batch of fondant. Afterward I washed my hands and wiped down the counter.

Cake-decorating wasn't much fun without Tony.

THE NOTE

On Friday I came downstairs and found a Sticky Note taped to the TV remote control. Dad puts notes for me and Sam there because he says then he's sure we'll see them. Which is true. Unless, of course, Bear decides to steal the remote. That's Sam's fault because he likes to eat while watching TV so there's always chip grease or peanut butter smeared on the remote. Bear was *my* fault. I was the one who begged for a puppy when our neighbor's dog had a litter. Her name was also my fault. With all that white fur, she reminded me of a miniature polar bear.

This is what Dad's note said:

Dear Thing One & Thing Two:

    Mom is at work. She's got a full shift and won't be home until dinnertime. I have classes until about four. I need you guys to pitch in:

- Wipe down the kitchen counter and load the dishwasher.
- Vacuum the whole house.
- Mow the lawn. (Sam, this means front <u>and</u> back!)
- Start the laundry.

I rolled my eyes at Bear who just cocked her head. Great. Cleaning was so *not* what I wanted to do.

I carried the note into the kitchen to save for Sam.

Someone had left a box of store-brand oatmeal on the counter. I put it away in the pantry, and then stood on a cooler to get the box of Peanut Butter Crunch. It was behind the flour on the top shelf, one of the few things Mom hadn't gone generic with yet. I didn't know why she bothered to hide it. It wasn't like Sam, Dad, and I didn't know it was there.

My pill and a cup of water were on the table, next to an empty bowl. I was trying a new brand of medicine. When Dad lost his job, we changed insurance companies who said we had to. It didn't seem to be working quite as well, but it was hard to tell. There was no real routine now because it was summer, and a routine helped.

I slouched into a chair, took my medicine, and ate the cereal right out of the box with my hand.

After breakfast I headed back to the living room and channel-surfed until I found a show about the world's most deadly insects. I watched it while I went through my student handbook for taekwondo.

The handbook wasn't really a book. It was one of those folders with three prongs. The first page was a diagram of how to properly tie our belts. The second page was a letter of introduction from Master Kim. It said we'd get an application and a list of the test requirements one belt at a time. Then after a test, we'd get another application and more papers to add to the folder. The third page listed my yellow-belt requirements, and the last page was the test application.

To get my yellow belt, I had to be able to block a punch and do a wrist escape, do a form called *kicho il bo*, and break a board with a push kick. I also had to be able to do the basic motions, which included kicks, punches, blocks, and stances, and to say them in Korean and count to ten in Korean, too. (I read through the numbers: *hana, dool, set, net, dasut, yasut, ilgop, yuldol, ahop, yul*.) And on top of all that, I had to know the definition of *taekwondo*.

This seemed like a lot to know all at once.

I shut the handbook, tossed it on the end table, and went back to channel-surfing.

Sam woke from the dead and came downstairs around ten-thirty. He was complaining about a missing shirt, and I hoped he wasn't going to stay an Oscar all day. (Oscar is what Mom called us when we were little and being grouchy.)

"Did you remember to take your medicine?" Sam asked before he grabbed the orange juice out of the fridge and drank it straight out of the carton.

"Yes," I grumbled. "Don't I always?"

"Not always," he said in an annoying way.

Just for that, I was glad I had finished off the Peanut Butter Crunch.

INSULT TO INJURY

Sam and I divvied up the chores. Well, we sort of divvied things up. It was more like Sam told me I was stuck with the kitchen and vacuuming.

"I'll do the laundry since we all know what happened last time *you* did it," Sam said.

If he wasn't a foot taller, I would have shoved him. It wasn't *my* fault a new red kitchen towel got mixed in with the whites. The stupid thing was already in the washing machine when I loaded the clothes.

I wiped down the counters and started unloading the dishwasher, but then I noticed it was time for *The Price Is Right* to come on so I took a break. A contestant who looked just like my preschool teacher won $10,000 playing Plinko. I wondered what I would do with that much money. I'd probably save it to put it toward opening The Tasty Pastry someday. Tony and I learned during our project that running a business was expensive.

When I was done watching the show, I found Sam on the computer. He had his e-mail account open, and his feet were keeping beat to the music coming from the computer. His driver's license study guide was lying open on the desk. And he was texting someone on his phone, his thumbs flying. (I got one of those pay-as-you-go phones for my birthday last year. But I lost it before I could get the hang of texting.)

Just looking at Sam made my brain jumpy. And that was even *with* my medicine. I took a deep breath and counted to sixteen like Mom taught me. Sixteen is four times four. And four is my all-time favorite number. It's the first even one with nice, straight lines. That's true whether you make it with an open or closed top.

Sam caught me looking at him. "What?" he said. The word came out like a giant sigh.

I glanced at the computer. I wanted to check my e-mail but didn't want to tell him that. I was afraid he'd say something mean, like, *Why? You never have e-mail. You need friends to get e-mail.*

"You better mow, or Dad'll be mad," I said.

Sam heaved another giant sigh like it was *my* fault Dad said he had to mow the front and backyards. "I'll do it after lunch."

"Then fix lunch," I said. "I'm hungry."

"Make your own cold hot-dog sandwich," he said, not even looking up from his phone.

His comment jabbed at my heart. Sam knew how much I liked the way he cut the two hot dogs into eight equal pieces. He even made my sandwich for me each day before school. I stood there, not knowing what to say next.

Sam stopped texting and looked up at me. "Fine," he said, putting his phone into his pocket. "I'll fix your sandwich."

"Thanks."

Sam unfolded himself from the chair and headed for the kitchen. "You're weird," he said as he walked past me.

People at school called me weird all the time, but I liked the way Sam said it. It was like he secretly thought I was cool.

BLANK

I sat down at the computer and logged on.

Nope. It'd been eleven days since Tony hung up on me for the second time. And there were still no e-mails. Or phone calls.

Nothing.

KICHO IL BO, CHA-CHA-CHA

On Saturday I was determined to ignore Madison completely. Thankfully she was in the front row, and I was in the third, so it was easy. I tried to pretend she was just some girl I knew from school. I was like, "Madison who? Oh yeah. I think we had art together one time. I can't remember."

I sat down and closed my eyes for meditation. The hum of the overhead florescent lights filled my head. I used to hate this part about taekwondo, but now I loved it. I know it sounds weird, but I imagined a cool white fog surrounding me. It made me feel peaceful, and I liked having the chance to think about what came next. Class always started the same way: We bowed; did meditation, warm-ups, and stretches; and then we ran through our basic motions before working on our skill for the day. It was predictable. And predictable was good.

When there were about twenty minutes of class left, Master Kim announced we'd be working on our forms.

"In the ancient days of martial arts, Masters created *poomsae*, or forms, as a way for students to practice their techniques. Today we carry on that tradition. Forms are a series of blocks, kicks, and punches set in a pattern. They are the foundation of taekwondo. Your form will be one of your requirements at your belt test in August."

The yellow, gold, and orange belts stood at the front of the room to practice with the teenage helpers. Even though I was trying to ignore her, my eyes were drawn to Madison. Her forms were so graceful and strong. She reminded me of a tiger. And you could tell that the other kids were peeking at her when they got stuck. They were gonna be sorry if they thought they could count on her to help them, though.

Master Kim came to the back of the room to work with the white belts. There were eight of us and somehow I ended up in the front row, smack in front of Master Kim. I was used to being in the back and kind of hidden. I'd forgotten how stern Master Kim looked up close. And with his hands behind his back, his feet planted under his shoulders, and his back straight, he looked like a soldier. I quickly forgot all about Madison.

"At each new belt level, you will have a form to learn," Master Kim explained. "The first form you'll be learning is *kicho il bo*. Say it. *Kicho il bo*."

I recited the name with the rest of the white belts. Then I kept reciting it inside my head. *Ki-cho il bo. Ki-cho il bo.*

It was fun to say, like a magic spell.

I focused as hard as I could on listening to Master Kim explain the first few steps. But by the time I figured out one move, he was already on the next one. Plus, I was supposed to be moving along some invisible line on the carpet. How was I possibly going to remember everything?

Master Kim stopped the group after a few more moves. "Good," he said. "Let's go through what we know so far one more time."

Instead of returning to the ready position, my feet stayed planted. I felt dread rolling up my back. I couldn't even remember what I was supposed to do first.

But then Master Kim put his hand up and told us to rest for a moment. He went to the front of the room and grabbed three long ropes. "This might make it easier," he said, laying the rope down on the floor.

"Every *poomsae* is made up of lines. *Kicho il bo*'s pattern looks like a capital letter *I*. See?"

On the ground was a giant capital *I* made out of ropes. Master Kim did the form slowly.

Lower block, step, punch. Turn. Lower block, step, punch. With each movement, I could hear the faint *snap* of his *dobok*. I watched his feet. It really was the letter *I*. I could see it!

Then Master Kim took us through the form a few times.

I kept forgetting to *kihap* when I was supposed to, but other than that, I got it. One, two, *kicho il bo*. One, two, *kicho il bo*.

It was kind of like a dance. A dance my arms and legs could do.

STUPID TONY AND HIS STUPID CHEF'S HAT

After we were dismissed, I went to the bathroom to change while Dad went to get the car. I couldn't get my itchy *dobok* off quick enough. Dad had been wrong; it hadn't softened up that much in the laundry.

I shoved my uniform into the bag, slipped on my flip-flops, and headed out the front doors.

And there he was, standing by the curb.

Tony.

He was spinning a chef's hat around his finger in the air. The kind of chef's hat *I* wanted. The chef's hat I would have gotten if Mom and Dad didn't think I was a quitter and had let me sign up for Cakes with Caroline.

Tony gave me a nod. "Hey, Eliza. What's up?"

"Hi." I tried to sound casual, even though my heart was pounding in my ears.

"So. Um. What are you doing here?" he asked.

"Taking a class," I said. I couldn't stop staring at the spinning chef's hat. I wanted to do two things at the same time: 1) Ask him if I could try it on; and 2) grab it out of his hand so he'd stop spinning it.

"Cool," Tony said. "I'm just hanging out. My mom's running late."

All kinds of thoughts began bumping around my brain, and every single one was trying to be the first in line: *We could give you a ride. I'm sorry. I'm still mad at you. Is the cake class fun? Wait. Don't tell me. What would you say if you I told you I'm taking taekwondo? Can I try on your chef's hat? Have you found a new partner to open a bakery with someday?*

But none of this is what I said.

"What's new?"

"Well, I'm going to try out for the basketball team in the fall," Tony told me.

This was news to me. I wondered if anything else had changed. "What about The Tasty Pastry?" I asked.

Tony looked confused. Then he asked, "What about it?"

"Aren't we still going to do it?" I tried my best to keep my voice calm, but it sounded squeaky.

Tony shrugged, and then his eyes searched the parking lot. His mom still wasn't there. "Okay," he finally said.

Okay what? Okay he heard me? Or okay we were still going to open our own shop someday?

Dad pulled up and honked. I stared at Tony, hoping I'd find a clue about what he meant, but his face was blank as a new notebook.

Dad honked again.

"I gotta go," I said.

"Right," Tony said. "See ya."

As I walked by him, I gave a little wave but kept my eyes at the ground.

"Wasn't that Tony?" Dad asked when I got into the car. "Does he need a ride?"

"No," I said.

Tony doesn't need anything, I thought miserably. *Including me*. I turned the vent toward my face so the cool air could keep the hot tears in my eyes from spilling. When I did, I bumped a Sticky Note off the dashboard.

"What's this one for?" I asked Dad, reattaching the note. I was desperate to change the subject.

"Oh. That," Dad answered. "Gotta get the car in. Brakes are squealing."

"You're like the king of Sticky Notes, huh?"

"Do monkeys have tails?" Dad teased.

"I can never remember," I said, forcing a smile. "Do they?"

This is an old family joke. Mom told me that when I was a toddler, Dad would hold me up in the air and pretend to look for my monkey tail because I liked to climb so much. Sam, who was six then, would laugh his head off. Dad stopped doing it when I got bigger.

Things change.

NOT AGAIN

We were a block from home, on our way to taekwondo, when Dad slowed down and signaled to turn into a random driveway.

"Shoot! I forgot my textbook," he said. "Gotta turn around."

"No!" I freaked out. "I'll be late."

Dad laughed and kept going. "Far be it from me to go against a girl sporting a *dobok*," he said.

I rolled my eyes. "I'm just a white belt, Dad."

"Yeah, but someday you could be a black belt," he said. "Then I'll *really* have to watch out."

Me? A black belt? I tried to imagine myself looking like Master Kim or the teenage-girl black belt who sometimes helped out in class. The idea was interesting and all, but I wasn't going to be around long enough to do that. I just had to get through the summer so I could prove that I wasn't a quitter. *I'm gonna be a cake-maker not a board-breaker,* I thought. And then smiled a little at my own cleverness.

At the community center, I took my spot in the back row. I saw Madison was near the front of the room. She glanced at me for a half second and then looked away and started talking to the girl next to her.

Master Kim strolled to the front and a tall orange belt started class. "Class, *charyut!*"

We all stood at attention.

"*Sabumnim kyoonyae,*" the orange belt said.

The week before, one of the teenagers told me that *sabumnim* meant "master."

I bent at the waist like everyone else and mumbled, "*Annyeon hashimnikka.*" It seemed like an awful lot of syllables for just "hello," but I liked the way it bounced around in my mouth. It was like a super ball inside a closed shower—not that I'm going to say how I know what a super ball thrown inside a shower does.

After we practiced doing front stances and blocks, Master Kim told us to pair up and make a line.

I turned to another white belt named Rosa. "Partners?" I asked.

I was relieved when she nodded.

I stood on the higher-rank side. Even though I was a

white belt, too, I was older. In fact, I'd lost most of my baby teeth. But I only kept track because losing them meant I had to get stupid braces at the end of July.

I wondered if braces were going to hurt as much as Sam said they would. I hoped I didn't have to wear rubber bands like that girl in my class. She had bands on the sides and in the front. She could barely open her mouth! And she had to reach her fingers in and take the rubber bands out every time she wanted to eat something. She'd leave them on the lunch table. It was *gross*.

Stop!

I took a breath and blinked. I was changing channels in my brain again. I hit the GO BACK button like I learned in Jitter Lunch Bunch.

Master Kim was emptying the equipment bag. "Come get a kicking paddle," he said.

After Master Kim showed us how to do back kicks again, we were supposed to practice them. Ten on each side.

Back kicks were tricky. They had about a hundred steps. First, you had to pivot on your front foot, look over your shoulder, and then pull the other leg up tight against your body before snapping it straight back. Plus, you had to remember to pull your toes back and hit the target with your heel. It was a lot to think about. *And* it made me super dizzy.

Just as Rosa and I were about to start, Master Kim came over.

"One moment please," he said.

My partner and I stopped.

"Eliza, switch places," he said, pointing down the line. "You and Madison are a better size match."

Mustard stains! I felt like ants just showed up to the picnic.

WAYS MADISON ANNOYED ME

1. When I got stuck counting, she jumped in and told me how to say six in Korean without even asking if I wanted help.
2. One of her back kicks hit my finger.
3. When it was my turn, she held the paddle too high, and I kept missing.
4. She reminded me to *kihap* about a billion times.

THE PART WHERE IT WENT FROM *T* TO WORSE

On Saturday, Dad and I were running late. The door to taekwondo was closed when I got there. I wondered if I should knock or just open it.

I pressed my ear to the door. People were moving around, and Master Kim was saying, "*Charyut!* Attention!"

Shoot muffins! I was late. If people were moving around, I'd missed meditation.

I rested my hand on the door handle for a second, took a deep breath, and pressed down.

The rest of the students were lined up, facing Master Kim, and standing at attention. I stepped inside, and the door closed itself behind me with a *whoosh click*.

A few heads turned my way and then quickly snapped forward. I could feel my ears burn.

Master Kim waved me to the front.

Every eyeball in the room was on me. It was like the time at school when I was balancing a full pencil cup on the back of my hand and it accidentally tipped over right in the middle of science class. I wanted to disappear then, too.

I stopped a few feet away from the first row. Master

Kim motioned to me again. My knees wobbling, I walked up to him and bowed.

Master Kim returned my bow and spoke in a clear, low voice. "A good martial artist is respectful. And being respectful means being on time. When you are late to class, you must ask for permission to join."

I tried to swallow, but it was hard since my throat was sand dry. "May I join class, sir?"

"You may," Master Kim said. "Do twenty push-ups and then join the back row."

Twenty push-ups? Ugh.

I went to the edge of the room and did my push-ups while Master Kim led the rest of the students through warm-ups. At least they weren't staring at me.

After we stretched, Master Kim told us to run some laps. I fell in line behind an orange belt and kept my eyes on his heels. After a lap, I noticed someone with long, easy strides pass me on the right. Madison. Just great.

You're doing this for a reason, I reminded myself. *Think CAKE.*

As I did my last lap, I glanced Master Kim's way. He was standing in the front of the room, holding a three-ring binder and writing something down. Maybe he was taking attendance.

Or maybe he was marking a great big, fat *T* for tardy next to my name.

We practiced kicks and blocks in the air, and afterward Master Kim told us to make a line in front of him. (I made sure I was as far away from Madison as possible.) Then he went to his equipment bag and pulled out a pair of black mitts. They reminded me of a catcher's glove.

"Sweet!" I heard the boy behind me say under his breath. His voice flipped a switch inside me and I got excited, too, even though I didn't know what was going on.

"We're going to work on punching," Master Kim told the class. He asked the black belt to show us the proper way to put our thumbs across the outside of our fingers. (Tucking them inside meant, apparently, a surefire trip to the ER for a busted thumb.) And then she showed us how to rotate our wrists the last second of the punch for maximum power.

Maximum power sounded cool. Like some kind of comic book hero. Don't worry. Max Power will save the day!

Master Kim put a mitt on each hand and held them up. When it was our turn, we were supposed to stand in fighting position, jab with our front hand, and then punch with our back hand and *kihap*. The line moved quickly.

When it was my turn, I took aim and threw my two punches.

Thud! Thud!

The punching mitts were harder than a catcher's glove. My knuckles hurt, but in a good way, if that makes sense.

I ran to the back of the line and bounced on my toes. I got two more turns, and each time it was: *Look out, mitts. Thud! Thud!*

When I got to the back of the line for the third time, my

hands and legs were twitchy with energy. I wanted to keep practicing, so I turned to the boy behind me and threw a few jabs and punches in the air at him.

"Eliza!" Master Kim's voice was sharp. Everyone froze.

"A word," Master Kim said as he motioned to the back of the room. He bowed, handed the mitts to the black belt, and asked her to take over.

I walked to the spot. My wobbly knees came back.

Master Kim put his hands behind his back and lowered his gaze until it sat like a brick on my head.

"Your martial-art skills are never to be used against an innocent person or in a playful manner," he said. "Is that clear?"

I wished I'd had a turtle shell on my back instead of a *dobok*. "Yes sir."

"If you forget, you will be asked to leave class and not allowed to return."

"Yes sir."

Master Kim pointed to the wall. "Take a seat. You need to sit out the rest of the drill."

My whole body deflated, and I slid down against the wall as Master Kim walked back to the front of the room.

A few of the kids snuck looks my way. I pretended not to see them and tried not to think about crying. But not thinking about crying is like not thinking about scratching an itch, and I had to sniff a few times.

Where was Max Power when you needed him?

ADIOS, MUCHACHOS

When I got home, I wadded up my *dobok* and threw it on the closet floor. Then I sat down on my bed. A sob bubbled up, but I swallowed it back.

Master Kim hated me.

Stupid Madison Green was in the class. Madison! The girl who put dumb swirls instead of dots over her "i's".

My *dobok* was still itchy.

I couldn't do any of the kicks the right way.

I was torturing myself for nothing. Tony was off, all happy in the cake class without me. He hadn't called or e-mailed or anything since we'd run into each other at the community center. That'd been over two whole weeks ago.

I don't care what Tony does. I don't care what Mom and Dad think!

And that's when I made the decision.

I quit.

MY NEW COAT

Mom says decisions are like coats because they weigh on your shoulders. So whenever Sam or I have a big decision to make, Mom says we should wear it for a while to see how it feels.

I put "quitting taekwondo" on and wore it for the rest of the afternoon. It felt good. So I decided to wear it to dinner, too.

I would present my case to Mom and Dad. They couldn't expect me to stick it out any longer. I wasn't a quitter. I really tried. I'd gone to five whole classes! That should count for something. I was just pursuing other options. The cake-decorating class was where I belonged. And maybe Tony's "okay" had been a good okay. Maybe opening our own bakery someday was still the plan.

I'd work on Dad first. He was usually the softie.

I took a breath and headed for the kitchen. Right off the bat there was a problem.

Dad wasn't there.

"Your father is at the library, studying," Mom said. (Mom called him "your father" when she was annoyed with him.)

I plunked down in the chair. Mom must have stopped at the grocery store and splurged on steaks and deli potato salad. But I wasn't hungry. That made me feel guilty on top of nervous.

I was going to tell her about quitting.

I was.

I'd worn the decision awhile like she said, and it felt right.

But when I was jabbing my fork at my salad, Mom said, "Eliza, I need your *dobok*. I'm doing a load of whites tonight."

I should have said, "I don't need it anymore. I've decided to pursue other options."

But that's not what I said. I said, "I'll bring it down later."

THAT'S WHEN I MADE ANOTHER DECISION

I'd tell Mom and Dad about quitting when they were together.

PLAN B

I didn't find Mom and Dad together on Sunday. I didn't find them together on Monday or Tuesday night, either.

On Wednesday morning, Mom didn't have to work, and Dad didn't have class until the afternoon. Mom made her famous chocolate-chip pancakes. Sam was still in bed.

It was just the three of us.

Time was running out. I had taekwondo class that afternoon. The moment was perfect, but now that it was here, the speech I'd rehearsed flew out of my head.

I'm quitting.

It was two words. No big deal.

Only I remembered. Dad had said, "Losers quit when they're tired. Winners quit when they've won." And Mom had laughed.

"You okay?" Dad asked.

"Yeah. You look a bit pale," Mom said. "I hope you're not coming down with something."

And that's when I suddenly decided to go to Plan C.

"My stomach kind of hurts," I said.

It wasn't a perfect plan. For one thing, Mom whisked away my pancakes before I could finish them. And I ended up on the couch for the entire day with a bucket next to me, which made me a little queasy for real. But I also got to sip on Sprite with a bendy straw. And Mom rubbed my feet before she got up to clean the bathrooms.

I wondered, *If I got mysteriously sick every Wednesday and Saturday would my parents notice?*

OKAY. SO HERE'S WHEN I WAS GONNA MAKE MY BIG ANNOUNCEMENT FOR REAL

1. When Mom and Dad were together.
2. And when Mom wasn't tired from work, and Dad wasn't grumpy from studying.
3. *And* when Sam wasn't around to tease me about being a loser quitter.
4. Later.

JULY FOURTH

It was a miracle. I made a complete recovery by Saturday. There was no taekwondo class because of the holiday, so my family went to the Yankee Doodle Doo-Dah at the local park.

The high-school drum line was performing at the festival, and Dad and I were on our way to hear Sam play. Mom was the official band nurse during marching season, so she went to help, in case someone passed out from the heat or dropped a drum on their toe.

As Dad and I snaked our way through the crowd, I heard a familiar voice: "*Charyut!*"

Master Kim was wearing his *dobok*, standing beside a large square of mats. On the mats were about a dozen students, including several black belts. I recognized one of the black belts. She helped out in class. I recognized one of the colored belts, too. Madison.

Master Kim had the group show off some kicks. One of them was crescent kick. Even though I'd never admit it to *her*, Madison was kind of awesome at it. Her leg swung up and around in front of her face like it was a whip. She could kick someone in the head if she wanted. No problem.

When the group was done with the kicks, the audience clapped. Then Master Kim told the crowd, "The black belts here today have trained for many years."

He held out two boards in front of him, and one of the black belts came onto the mats. I recognized her from class. Her name was Abigail. She moved the boards up a little higher and stared them down like they were an enemy. And then she stepped into fighting position and—"*Yah!*"—broke the boards with her palm. The crowd oohed and clapped again.

"Come on, Eliza," Dad said as he tugged on my elbow. "We gotta go. The band will be starting soon."

"Just a sec," I said.

Dad checked his watch, which was his way of agreeing without actually agreeing.

Master Kim had two boys get down on their hands and knees, side by side. Abigail walked away until she was about fifteen feet from them. Master Kim went to the other side of the boys and stood four or five feet away. He crouched in a deep front stance and held out a board in front of his chest.

The black belts on the ground lowered their heads.

Master Kim turned his head away.

The crowd grew quiet.

Abigail took a deep breath and stared at the board so hard that it looked like she was trying to break it with her mind. Then she let out a sharp *ha!* and was off, running straight toward the board.

Right before she got to the first boy, Abigail turned into a flying ninja. Her front leg shot out, and her back leg tucked up under her body. She was like a human arrow. When her front heel struck the board she let out another *ha!* and the board cracked in two. I clapped along with the crowd.

My first thought was: *Did she really just do that?*

My second thought was: *I wish I could do that.*

My third thought was: *Oh, yeah. I'm quitting.*

LET THERE BE CAKE

After we listened to Sam play, Dad and I headed toward Harrison Hall, the air-conditioned building on the edge of the park. (Mom hung back to help one of the drummers who was stung by a bee.) *This* is what I'd been waiting for all day. Every year the community festival held the Let There Be Cake contest for amateur bakers from 4:00 to 6:00. The community got to vote for the fan favorite. Unfortunately you had to be over eighteen to enter.

As we walked in, the cool air made my hot, sweaty skin tingle. The smell of frosting was pure heaven, and I'm pretty sure I did a happy sigh without thinking about it because Dad looked at me and grinned. Everywhere you looked, there were tables covered with cakes.

The tables were grouped by category. I lost track of how many. There were wedding cakes, birthday cakes, crooked cakes, character cakes (someone had made a three-headed Fluffy dog from Harry Potter!), cakes shaped like real-life objects, and regular round cakes.

My favorite category was Miniature Cakes. They weren't cupcakes but small-scale versions of cakes. And they were amazing! I had a hard time choosing which one to vote for. In the end, I picked the one that looked like a doll-size pink top hat with a blue and green butterfly sitting on top. The fondant was perfectly smooth. Around the brim, the baker had put pea-size balls of frosting painted like pearls.

But what was really neat about the mini-hat cake was that it was missing a slice. And inside there were seven mini-layers—each in a different color of the rainbow! It must have taken the baker forever to figure out how to do that just right.

I wondered which cake Tony would vote for. I knew his parents were helping judge the contest. But I hadn't seen them. Or him. When we made up (sooner or later), Tony and I would have to plan out what kinds of cakes we'd make in our shop. I hoped he liked the idea of a rainbow-layer one.

Dad said we could come back after dinner to see who won. Then he said he needed to use the restroom before we left.

"I'll just get a drink and wait for you," I told him.

There was a fountain near the restrooms. I stood behind a mother as she took turns holding her three kids up to get some water. All the kids looked younger than six. They were cute. A little cranky, though. But that was understandable. Crowds make me cranky, too, sometimes. I made a silly face at the littlest kid to try to get him to laugh.

The mother turned to me. "I'm sorry this is taking so long," she said to me with a weary smile.

"It's okay," I told her. "I'm not in any hurry."

"Now *that's* refreshing!" someone behind me said.

There was something about the woman's voice that was familiar. I turned around and nearly fainted dead away. It was Sweet Caroline! She was wearing a dazzling smile and badge that said JUDGE.

"A lot of young people today have given up on common courtesy," she said, looking right at me.

Sweet Caroline was standing here. Talking to *me*.

My brain was a jar of marbles that someone had just spilled on the floor. I tried to grab one of the thoughts rolling around so I could say something.

"Your show is my favorite," I said.

Sweet Caroline's smile got even more dazzling as she extended her hand. "Why, thank you!" she said. "I love meeting fans."

I shook her hand. It was small and soft.

"I'm sorry I can't stay and chat," Sweet Caroline said. "I'm judging the contest. Have you voted for your favorite yet?"

I told her that I had.

"Wonderful! Well, enjoy the rest of your day."

"Thank you," I said. "You too."

As Sweet Caroline walked away, she waved. "Remember," she said. "Be sweet . . ."

". . . to everyone you meet!" I called after her.

She laughed, which made me feel light as angel-food cake.

OPERATION
NEW PLAN

Stretched out in bed that night, I thought of a hundred things I could have said to Sweet Caroline. And I came up with a hundred different ways our meeting could have ended. Like Sweet Caroline inviting me to help judge and us running into Tony and him being jealous.

I also thought about the rainbow-layered cake. The baker must have spent a lot of time practicing. Just like Flying Ninja Girl had to. It must have taken her years of training to do that cool board break.

Hmm.

Had I really put in enough time at taekwondo? I was pretty sure Mom and Dad wouldn't think so.

Now that I knew for sure Sweet Caroline would like me, I wanted to take her class even more. If that was possible.

And there was only one way to do that.

JUST LIKE THAT

I made sure I was early to class the following week. And even though most of the kids were hanging out, talking or practicing, I spent the few minutes figuring out who I was supposed to stand next to when class started so I could line up right away. I needed to make a good impression. At least Madison wasn't in class. Maybe she'd gone on vacation for the rest of the summer. I could only hope.

I wondered if Master Kim would still be mad at me. It's not like I'd never been in trouble before. In fact, I got into trouble at school a lot when I was younger. But I never got used to it. I knew most of my old teachers didn't like having me in class much. I could tell because when I walked into the classroom their mouths would say, "I'm glad you're here!" But their eyes said it wasn't true.

I wondered what Master Kim's eyes would say.

Speaking of Master Kim, he marched into the room at that precise moment. His voice boomed, "Class, *jong yul*! Line up!"

I scrambled to my spot in the third row and willed myself not to look at him.

When he was about halfway to the front, Master Kim stopped. "Eliza," he said.

My heart skidded to a halt.

I forced myself to look up. "Yes . . . yes sir?"

Master Kim gave a little nod. "Please tighten your belt."

I glanced down at my loose belt knot and then quickly back at Master Kim. "Yes sir."

His mouth was a straight line, but his eyes were bright.

I turned to the back of the room like I was supposed to and fixed my belt. When I turned back around, Master Kim was at the front of the room and asking the orange belt in the corner to bow us in.

Just like that. It was class as usual.

GREAT INSTINCT

We practiced our forms. Even though it had been over a week since I last did my form, I remembered almost all of the steps. At the top of the *I*, I started to turn the wrong way, but at the last second I fixed it. *Kicho il bo*, cha-cha-*cha*.

When the white belts were done, we sat along the wall. I liked watching the other kids do their forms. Each form had a different name and meaning. The yellow belts did one called *taeguk il jang*.

"Who can tell me what this form represents?" Master Kim asked.

A girl on the end of the second row raised her hand and answered, "The great principle of Heaven."

The great principle of Heaven.

That sounded much nicer than "basic form number one," which is what Master Kim said *kicho il bo* translated to.

When everyone was done with their forms, we moved on to our board breaks. Since there was an odd number of students, one of the black belts came over to be my partner. It was Abigail, also known as Flying Ninja Girl from the Fourth of July. I wanted to ask her how long it took her to learn to do the board break and if it was as fun as it looked, but she told me to get a kicking paddle.

"Yes ma'am," I said. (It still felt really weird to call a teenager ma'am.)

Abigail bowed and took the paddle from me. "What's your board break?"

"Push kick," I said.

She held the paddle up. "Okay. Go ahead and give it a shot."

I moved back until I thought I was a good distance and then stepped back into my fighting stance.

I lifted my back leg, pulled it close, and shot out my foot.

My kick was weak.

"*Kihap* next time," Abigail said.

I tried again, this time remembering to yell. The kick felt better, but Abigail said it probably wouldn't have broken a board.

She put her free hand a few inches behind the paddle. "Trying kicking my hand."

After a few more tries, Abigail stopped me. "You're stopping at the paddle," she said. "Kick past it."

Great. Now she was talking in Yoda-eese like Master Kim.

Maybe I'd been too hasty about coming back.

No!

I had to do this. *Think CAKE*, I told myself.

"*Koomahn.* Stop," Master Kim called out from the middle of the room. Everyone turned their attention to him. "I need two students."

I inched behind Abigail. But Master Kim called me and Mark over.

Oh applesauce.

"We're going to learn how to sidestep a kick," Master Kim told the class. Then he demonstrated the technique. When one person threw a roundhouse kick, the other person was supposed to move at an angle to the right. At the same time, the second person was supposed to block the kick and throw a punch to the person's chest.

Master Kim asked me to throw a roundhouse with my back leg. Mark sidestepped perfectly.

"Now you try," Master Kim said to me.

At least that's what I think he said. It was hard to tell with my heart beating in my ears.

Mark kicked.

I moved.

Only instead of stepping to the side like I was supposed to, I slid backward. It was just enough for the kick to miss me.

Mark looked confused, and my heart sank. I'd messed up. In front of everyone!

"Did everyone see what Eliza did?" Master Kim asked.

I wished my oversized *dobok* would just swallow me up on the spot.

"What Eliza just did is called a *whojin*," Master Kim told everyone. "And it's a good way to avoid an attack."

I blinked.

I'd done something good? I felt my back straightening.

Master Kim turned to me and gave me a nod. "You showed great instinct, Eliza."

NOT THAT I NEEDED THEM

In the back of the room, there was a box of extra equipment Master Kim said we could take. I waited until everyone else was gone and checked it out. I didn't really need anything since I wasn't staying in taekwondo past summer, but I grabbed a pair of arm pads and a pair of leg pads anyway.

THE A

On Thursday night, Mom picked up a pizza for dinner.

"So," she said as she passed out paper plates. "Is there any news that's fit to print?" That's her way of asking if anything interesting happened during the day. I don't know why she just doesn't ask it the normal way.

I shrugged. I'd spent most of the day watching a cartoon marathon and going through a whole bottle of nail-polish remover and two bottles of polish. I couldn't quite mix the exact shade of green I wanted.

"I reached the fifth level of *Zombie Bounty Hunters*," Sam said.

"I'm guessing that's a good thing," Mom said with a laugh.

"Well, I got a bit of good news today," Dad announced. "Remember that big paper I had to write for my child psychology class? I got an A."

We all whooped and clapped and gave Dad high fives.

"This calls for a celebration," Mom said. "I think there's some ice cream in the freezer."

"You know what I'd really like?" Dad asked. "A cake. Eliza, will you make me one?"

"Do monkeys have tails?" I asked.

"I can never remember," Dad teased. "Do they?"

After dinner Dad and I went to the grocery store to get stuff to make a chocolate cake with buttercream frosting. Dad put the Jeep's top down. The two of us love doing this on summer nights. You can lean your head back and see the whole navy sky, feel the warm air on your skin, and hear all the traffic around you. Mom and Sam prefer closed windows and air-conditioning.

"The Jeep reminds me of riding a roller coaster," I told Dad as we drove down the road.

Dad laughed. "It reminds me of being twenty-two, fresh out of college," he said. "I saved up for this car for four years. It was the last impractical thing I bought before I became a grown-up."

I couldn't picture my dad as a twenty-two-year-old man. Or as a kid. I wondered if he was the kind of boy who was nice, like Tony. Or if he was mean, like David Ruckers, who called me a hyperhen when I couldn't sit still in math class 'cause I'd forgotten my medicine that morning.

"Dad," I asked. "When you were my age, did you want to be an architect?"

Dad chuckled. "Nope. When I was your age, I didn't even know what an architect was."

"Then why did you become one?"

"Well, when I was in college, I *thought* I wanted to."

I considered his answer.

Dad went on. "The thing is, Eliza, sometimes we don't really know what we want. We just think we do."

I was quiet for a minute before I asked my next question. "Do you wish you were still one? An architect, I mean."

Dad kept his eyes on the road but knitted his brow. "Yes

and no," he said. "I wish I had a steady job so I could afford all the things you, Sam, and your mom want. But no, it wasn't a good job for me. It didn't make me happy."

"Do you think being a teacher will make you happy?" I asked.

"Yes," Dad said with a smile. "I do."

I knew exactly what would make me happy. To make cakes with Tony at our own shop.

BLUE

I grabbed a basket while Dad took out our list. Mom learned long ago to never send me and Dad to the store without a detailed list. "The two of you are dangerous together," she said. "It's like the blind leading the blind!"

She's right. One time Dad and I went out to buy a snow shovel before a big storm and came back with two movies, a jigsaw puzzle, and a couple of beanbag chairs. But no shovel.

The baking stuff was in aisle six. I started grabbing what we needed, and Dad followed behind me. "Go for it," he said, holding up the basket. I took aim and tossed a bag of M&M'S right in.

"Nothing but net!" Dad said.

A gray-haired lady nearby shook her head at him, but Dad kept smiling this goofy "Who me?" smile. He was gonna be a great teacher.

While we were checking out, I asked Dad if I could have money for a Slushie. He handed me a five, and I headed over to the service counter, where the Slushie machine was.

Just as I started filling the plastic cup with blue raspberry, I heard giggling. I looked up and saw Madison and two of her friends tagging behind one of their moms. The mom walked up to the counter to return something. Madison and the girls wandered over to a claw-machine game in the corner.

My nerves tingled, but I concentrated on pulling the Slushie-machine handle and the blue liquid filling my cup. Had Madison and her friends seen me? Maybe they hadn't. I couldn't help it. I dared a quick look their direction. Madison was playing the game, but the other two girls were looking at me and whispering.

I tried to remember all the things I'd ever been told about how to deal with people being jerks. *Just ignore them.*

I looked away, but then I swear I heard someone say, "Every day." The whispering turned into laughter.

My throat hurt. *Don't cry! Don't give them the satisfaction.*

My Slushie cup was full so I reached over and grabbed a straw. I knew I should grab a lid, too, especially since we'd come in Dad's bumpy Jeep, but I just wanted to get out of there as fast as I could.

I walked away. I don't know why, but I glanced in the girls' direction one more time. Madison was saying something to the other girls.

It was weird. She looked kind of mad.

PULLING A ME

Forty minutes later, the oven was hot, and I was standing at the counter, measuring out ingredients. I tried to follow the recipe in the cookbook but kept thinking about Madison and her stupid friends instead.

Crack went the first egg. I threw the shell in the sink.

Sam marched up to the sink to fill his glass.

I grabbed the second egg. *Crack*.

"Hey E. What're ya doing?" he asked.

I stared as the egg yolk and white slid down the disposal. I couldn't believe it. I'd cracked the egg into the sink instead of the mixing bowl!

"Ha! You pulled an Eliza!'" Sam said.

I snapped my head his direction. "You're not supposed to use that expression anymore," I said through gritted teeth. I could feel hot tears fill my eyes.

"Yeah. Okay," he said, throwing his free hand up in the air in surrender. "Don't freak."

Freak.

I'd heard that before, too.

My throat felt achy again. Like someone was squeezing it.

I went to the bathroom, splashed cool water on my face, and blew my nose. I didn't look in the mirror, though. Whenever I was upset, seeing my own splotchy red face made me sadder.

Forget about those mean girls, I told myself. *They're not important.*

A CAKE ONLY A DAD COULD LOVE

So it turns out decorating a cake is hard when your medicine is wearing off and your brain is speeding up.

You have to put on a crumb layer first, which is a thin layer of frosting where all the crumbs get caught. It doesn't matter how it looks because afterward you put the pretty layer of frosting on top. You're supposed to put your cake in the refrigerator after you do the crumb layer so it can get hard. But I didn't have time because it was already getting late. I had to put on the top layer right away and crumbs got mixed in. To make matters worse, the cake was also slightly tilted because part of it got stuck when I dumped it out of the pan.

I took a step back and studied my cake.

It reminded me of when Tony and I made a sheet cake as part of our project. Since Tony was a huge fan of Halloween, we made one that looked like a graveyard. It had scary trees, tombstones, and zombies made out of modeling chocolate. But we'd made it at my house and our old oven didn't bake the cake evenly. (Tony's family bakery had some big last-minute order so we couldn't make the cake there.) Parts of the cake were done, and parts were gooey. It was a mess. I was disappointed and ready to make a new one, but Tony just scooped out the gooey parts and we turned them into dug-up graves. "It's our *monster*piece! Get it?" he'd said.

I'd laughed, and Tony put his arms out in front of himself and started moaning. I pretended to be a zombie, too. We kept moaning, "Brains. Braaaaains," and laughed until our sides ached.

I sighed.

Fixing Dad's cake wasn't as much fun without Tony. But I had to come up with something, so I covered the whole thing with another layer of frosting. That hid most of the crumbs. Next I used M&M'S to spell out way to go, dad! In the end, it wasn't great; but it was decent.

When I let everyone back into the kitchen to show it off, Dad broke into a huge grin. "I love it!"

"You did a good job, honey," Mom said.

"Yeah," Sam added. "It's not completely terrible. I'll get a knife."

I ignored the dork and looked at Mom. And then, as casually as I could, I said, "Just think how good I'll be after I take Sweet Caroline's class in the fall."

"We'll see," Mom said. "You have to hold up your end of the bargain first."

"Yeah," Dad added. "A deal's a deal."

WHY I WAS UP AT 12:14 A.M.

Later that night, my brain wouldn't shut down; but I was used to it.

I lay in bed and used my nightlight to count the photos on my bulletin board (twenty-four). Then I tried to memorize their order from top to bottom. But what had happened earlier kept replaying in my head.

What Mom and Dad said bothered me. I had to show them that I wasn't a quitter.

I kicked off my sheet and crept out of bed. I needed to look through my taekwondo handbook again. I couldn't remember what all the test requirements were.

I checked my middle desk drawer, but the handbook wasn't there. I looked in the suitcase where I kept my books. It wasn't there, either. Or on top of my dresser.

Nougat. Where did I put it? My test application and all my memorization stuff was in it.

I was standing smack in the middle of my room, trying to decide where to look next when my door creaked. There was no time to dive back into bed.

"Eliza, what are you doing up?" Mom whispered from the doorway. "It's after midnight."

"Nothing," I whispered back.

"Can't you sleep, sweetie?" Mom asked. "Do you want a melatonin pill?"

"No, that's okay," I told her. "I . . . I just forgot to turn on my fan."

"It was kind of hot today, wasn't it," Mom said. She stepped over the pile of clothes and walked over to the fan. "Climb into bed. I'll turn it on for you."

When she was done, Mom came over and started to tuck me in.

"I'm too old," I told her.

"Oh. Okay." She sounded kind of sad. "G'night then," she said as she stood up and headed for the door.

I didn't mean the tucking-in thing in a mean way. I thought about going down the hall to her bedroom and giving her one more kiss good-night. But then I remembered why I couldn't sleep. And why I was up looking for my missing handbook. And that I had to pass a yellow-belt test in August. And it was all because Mom and Dad thought I was a quitter.

So instead of going down the hall, I rolled over and listened to the *whirrrr* of the fan.

BAD NEWS, GOOD NEWS, DAD-WRECKED-THE-CAR NEWS

When Dad came home from school on Friday, the first thing he did was throw his bag on the kitchen table. Hard. It got Sam's attention all the way upstairs.

"Hey, Spaz! Stop knocking down the house," he called.

"It wasn't me!" I yelled at the ceiling. "Dad's home."

"For Pete's sake. Will you two lower the volume already?" Dad said. This was the second time in the last week Dad had come home grumpy.

Sam came crashing down the stairs. "Hey, Dad. Can I go to a movie? I need some money, too."

"How come he gets money and I don't?" I asked.

"Why should you get any money?" Sam said. "You never do your chores."

"I do them more than you do yours," I shot at him.

"Enough!" Dad shouted. "Knock it off, you two!"

Sam and I clammed up. Mom was more of the yeller in the family. (And it took *a lot* to get her angry.)

Dad waved a hand at us. "Sorry, guys. It's been a stressful day."

"What happened?"

I hated that Sam asked first.

"My car's toast," Dad said.

Sam ran to the front door and opened it while Dad and I stood in the kitchen. "Where is it?" Sam asked. "Did you wreck it?"

Wreck? I searched Dad for visible injuries. "Are you okay?" I asked.

"Don't worry. I'm fine," Dad said as Sam came back into the room. "And the car's at the mechanic. A friend from school brought me home."

Dad explained that he'd taken his car in to get looked at because the brakes were making noises. The mechanic told him the brake pads were completely gone. If Dad had brought the car in when the brake light first came on, it would have been easy to replace the pads. But now it was going to cost a lot more money. And since Mom didn't get paid until the end of the month, we didn't have the money to have it fixed right away.

"It's my own fault," Dad said. "I wrote myself a note weeks ago to have them looked at. I just got busy and forgot."

"When am I going to practice driving?" Sam asked.

Dad shrugged. "At night, I guess."

"How are you going to get to school?" I asked.

"Mom and I will have to work something out," Dad said.

"How am I going to get to taekwondo?" I said.

"Don't worry," Dad said. "I've got a ride all lined up for

you on the days Mom needs the car. I think you're even friends with the other girl." Dad smiled. "Her name is Madison."

ARG

It was bad enough I had to be in the same room with Madison. Now I had to be in the same *car* with her.

Peach pits.

COOKIE

The next afternoon, I still couldn't believe it. I was stuck riding to taekwondo with Madison just because Dad forgot to take his car in for repair when the brake light came on. He'd written himself a note. I saw it myself! This was all his fault.

Madison was in the front seat. (Thank the stars.) A pile of department-store bags took up half of the back seat. I climbed into the car and shoved my gym bag at my feet. Madison gave me a weak hello, and I muttered one back.

"Thanks for giving me a ride, Mrs. Green," I said to Madison's mother, remembering Dad's instructions.

"Oh, please, sweetheart. Call me Cookie!"

I wondered if that was her real name or a nickname. But I figured it might be rude to ask so I just said, "Um. Okay."

Cookie gave me a sparkly toothy grin in the rearview mirror, turned up the radio, and backed out of my driveway.

I was glad the music was loud because that way I didn't have to talk to Madison. The two of us looked out our windows while Cookie sang along to songs on WQFM80.5, the Awesome Eighties All-the-Time station.

At a red light, Madison's mother turned down the radio and declared, "My heavens. You two are awfully quiet."

When Madison and I didn't respond, Cookie kept talking. "So, Eliza. Are you looking forward to starting middle school?"

I lied and told her I was. Adults never want to hear the truth about these kinds of things anyway.

"You're lucky," Cookie said. "Madison is *so* nervous about it."

I was surprised. After all Madison had plenty of friends and always made the honor roll.

Cookie glanced over at Madison. "Speaking of which, when are we going shopping for your back-to-school clothes? Things are on sale now, and you obviously didn't like what I picked out for you."

Cookie threw a disgusted look at the bags in the backseat when she said this last part.

"That's because you pick out ugly stuff," Madison said.

"Well, forgive me for trying to spoil my only daughter

and broaden her fashion horizons," Cookie said in that I'm-teasing-but-I'm-really-kinda-mad way parents sometimes do.

Madison sighed. "I like the clothes I have."

"Don't be ridiculous," Cookie said. "You can't very well go to school wearing the same thing day after day."

I looked down at my shorts and used my hand to cover a stain. *Every Day Eliza* popped into my head.

Madison and her mom stopped talking.

Cookie gave up on Madison and came back to me. "So, Eliza. Are you going to try out for any teams or do any clubs in middle school?"

I wasn't, but Mom said answering just "yes" or "no" was rude. So I said, "I haven't decided yet."

"Maddie Pie hasn't decided yet, either," Cookie said.

The back of Madison's neck turned pink. "Mooomm!"

"What?" Cookie asked. "The name? Oh, for goodness' sake. I'm sorry."

Cookie sat up straighter and looked in the rearview mirror with a grin. "You didn't hear that, right, Eliza?"

"No," I said. (What else was I supposed to say?)

"See. No need to be embarrassed," Cookie said. "Besides, if you want to be embarrassed about something, it should be giving up cheerleading to concentrate on a sport like tae-kwondo." Cookie winced. "No offense, Eliza," she said in a cheerful voice.

Madison looked at her mom and opened and closed her mouth a few times, kind of like a goldfish. But in the end, she didn't say anything. I was too surprised to say anything, either.

Hadn't Cookie ever seen Flying Ninja Girl break a board or watched Master Kim go through a form perfectly? And didn't she know how *good* Madison was at it?

Cookie went back to singing with the radio, and Madison and I went back to listening to her in silence.

"Have fun, you two," Cookie said when she dropped us off. "I've got some returns to make. I'll be back in an hour."

As Cookie pulled away, Madison looked at me and then down at her flip-flops. "Sorry about what my mom said. She thinks taekwondo is for boys."

Madison Green just *apologized* to *me* for something. *Who is this?* I wondered. Sometimes people have evil twins. Maybe Madison had a nice twin instead.

I was so shocked, I just shrugged my bag higher up on my shoulder. "That's okay," I said. "I have a mom, too."

Madison looked up and gave me a half smile. "Thanks," she said.

MY MOM HAS NO IMAGINATION

A couple of days later, I decided to practice my push kick. I still couldn't find my handbook. And I was getting a little panicked. But at least I could work on my board break for my test. It wasn't very satisfying to kick the air: I couldn't tell if I was landing my foot on the imaginary target either so I improvised.

After I got tired of practicing my push kick, I decided to try a flying side kick like I'd seen the black belt do at the demo. But I found out *wanting* to do something isn't anywhere near *being able* to do something. It's probably best not to ask exactly how I found this out. Or how I know that Mom has no imagination and strenuously believes mattresses are for going on beds and not up against walls.

MALL, SHMALL

I was playing sock tug-of-war with Bear when Mom walked into the living room.

"The stores are having a Tuesday two-for-one sale," she said. "Are you up for some shopping and lunch?"

I wasn't all that crazy about the mall. Too many people,

too many choices, and too much noise. But I needed some plain white underwear for taekwondo days and wanted to look for a birthday present for Tony. Plus, it'd been forever since Mom and I had done something together.

"We could have lunch at that Chinese restaurant you like," she said in a singsongy way. "Crab rangoons."

One whole day alone with Mom. And rangoons.

"I'm in," I told her.

Right before we backed out of the garage, Mom put the car in park and unclipped her seat belt. "Oops. I forgot my phone, and I'm on call. I'll be right back."

On call. It figured. It seemed that even when Mom wasn't working, she was on call.

When we got to the mall, Mom wanted to look for new tennis shoes she'd heard other ER nurses raving about. We went into a few places, and I got stuck sitting on the bench while Mom wandered down the rows of shoes looking for the right brand.

"What do you think?" Mom asked as she modeled a pair of super-ugly tennis shoes.

"They're fine," I said.

Mom studied my face for a bit. Then she yanked off the shoes and put them back into the box.

"All right," she said. "Ditching my errand. Let's go do yours." She was trying to sound cheerful but I could tell she was annoyed.

Good.

In the underwear section, I pretended to be looking at

some socks while Mom went through the underwear packages. "What size do you wear, Eliza?"

"I dunno," I told her.

Even though I don't think she was supposed to, she opened a package and took out a pair of underwear. She walked over and held them up to my waist. "I think these will work," she said.

I stepped away as fast as I could. "Mooomm!" An older lady walked by and smiled.

"Relax," Mom said. "It's no big deal. Everyone wears underwear."

Relax. That was easy for Mom to say. She saw kids' underwear all the time when they came into the emergency room. Bodies were no big deal to her.

I pointed to the white underwear she was holding. "Those are good," I said. "Can I go wait outside while you pay?"

THE PART WHERE
I WAS COOL

There were leather chairs just outside the store by the escalators. I plopped down on one and waited for Mom.

"You guys stay here," a familiar girl's voice said. "I'll be right back. I mean it. Don't go anywhere."

I turned my head and saw Tony, his sister, and some guy I didn't know.

Tony's sister ducked into the coffee shop. Tony and his friend headed over to the seats, shoving each other off balance and laughing like it was the funniest thing in the world.

When he got a few feet away, Tony noticed me. "Oh, hey," he said. I couldn't tell if he was happy to see me or surprised or what.

"Hi," I said.

The kid next to Tony snickered and punched his shoulder. "Who's your girlfriend?"

Tony looked as uncomfortable as I felt. "Uh. This is just Eliza," he said. "*Not* my girlfriend."

I turned to the stranger. "Who are you?"

"This is Kevin," Tony said. "He's on the basketball team."

"Did you go to a different school?" I asked Kevin. He didn't look familiar.

"He's gonna be an eighth-grader," Tony explained.

An eighth-grader? Wow. I guess I shouldn't have been surprised. Everyone liked Tony. He was cool.

He didn't look so cool at the moment, though. Tony shifted from foot to foot and kept looking back and forth between me and Kevin. Why was he nervous?

It suddenly occurred to me Tony was trying to impress Kevin. Trying out for the basketball team was really important to Tony, and maybe Kevin was helping him practice.

Maybe Tony thought I'd do something embarrassing. He'd never cared what people said about me before, but maybe it was different now.

I decided to show him he had nothing to worry about. I could act casual. That's what friends did in a pinch. Even friends who were mad at each other.

"So how's the taekwondo class going?" Tony asked.

I shrugged. (Shrugging was casual. Right?) "Good," I said. "How 'bout your class?"

"It's fun," Tony said. "Um, anything else interesting going on?" he asked.

"Nope." I was so proud of myself for not rambling on about the miniature cakes and seeing Sweet Caroline at the festival.

Tony looked around. "You here by yourself?" he asked.

I pretended to be looking at something over his shoulder. "I'm waiting for my mom."

Tony motioned to Kevin. "We're waiting for my sister."

I stopped myself from saying I already knew that. See. I could be cool when I needed to be. This was going so well! I hoped Tony appreciated it.

Kevin sighed. "Come on," he said as he tugged on Tony's sleeve. "Let's go down and get samples at the cheese shop before your sister comes back."

Tony hesitated and looked at me. "Well, see ya," he said.

I tried to remember what Sam and his friends said when they were saying good-bye to each other. "Whatever,"

I said. As soon as it was out of my mouth, I knew the word I was really looking for was *later*. But I hoped it was close enough. I'd tell Tony I was sorry for messing it up when I went to his birthday party.

Tony let Kevin pull him onto the escalator. Right before the two of them disappeared, I got a glimpse of Tony's face. I don't know why, but something about his expression made me feel sad.

RANGOONS AND RAIN CHECKS

Mom came out of the store a few minutes later. "Ready for lunch?"

The Chinese restaurant in the mall was one of my favorite places to eat. The walls were red, and dozens of white paper lanterns hung from the ceiling. It also had the best crab rangoons in the world.

We beat the lunch crowd, so Mom and I were seated right away. We got a double order of rangoons. "We probably won't be hungry for our actual lunches after these," Mom said when the plate arrived.

"I'll give you a dollar if you can pick up a rangoon with your chopsticks," Mom challenged me. "*And* eat it before it drops."

I smiled. "You're on." I was a pro with chopsticks, and Mom knew it.

I got it on the first try. "Ha!" I said. "Pay up." Mom laughed and pulled out her wallet.

"Here," she said. "Milk money."

I was confused.

Mom rolled her eyes. "Sheesh," she said. "Way to make me feel old. Milk money is what kids used to buy their milk at school before lunch debit cards," she explained.

"Oh, okay," I said. Mom and I finished the appetizers.

The milk money thing got me worrying about middle school again. Maybe this was the perfect time to talk to Mom about it. It was just the two of us. No Sam to tease me about being a baby or Dad to give me a pep talk about how making friends was easy if you would just be yourself. How were you supposed to be yourself if no one liked the real you?

"Mom—?"

The server walked over with our tray. "Be careful," she said, setting down our entrees. "The plates are warm."

I was about to try again when Mom's phone chirped. She flipped it open and read the text.

"E. I'm so sorry," she said. "Apparently the ER is swamped, and I gotta go in."

"What about lunch?" I said.

"I guess we'll have to wrap it up and take it home," Mom said. "I'll make it up to you soon. Rain check?"

"Sure," I said. "If you say so."

"I'm on call, sweetie," Mom said. "I don't have a choice."

"Yeah. Okay," I said as flatly as I could. I knew she hated it when I did that.

Mom's face hardened. "Please don't be this way, Eliza."

"How am I supposed to be?" I knew I was whining but didn't care.

"You're old enough to understand," Mom said. "The hospital needs me."

I bit my bottom lip to stop it from trembling.

*But **I** need you, too*, I thought.

TO-DO LIST

When I got home, I took one of Dad's Sticky Notes and wrote my own to-do list. Then I put it on the inside of my closet door.

1. Keep giving Mom the silent treatment until she notices I'm not talking to her.
2. Practice push kick and GET A NEW HANDBOOK!
3. Survive a couple more rides with I-dot-my-*i*'s-with-swirls Madison.
4. Decide what to get Tony for his birthday.

BAD TIMING

After the first ride, I didn't think Madison and I were suddenly friends; but I was still surprised when she didn't say anything other than hello on the way to class the next day.

She and Cookie were scowling, too. I decided to pretend I was invisible.

I adjusted the backseat air-condition vent. It was too hot to move, let alone be wearing a long-sleeved *dobok*. Ugh. Master Kim said wearing the uniforms was tradition. But I still wished we could wear T-shirts and shorts.

My bangs were dripping by the time Master Kim told us to pair up for drills. I tried to catch Rosa's eye, but I didn't move fast enough and ended up with Mark instead.

We practiced blocking punches. It didn't go well.

Each time Mark threw a punch, I tried to knock his arm out of the way like I was supposed to. But I messed up every single time. My brain could see the punches coming. I just couldn't get the message to my arm fast enough. I was always half a second behind.

"Here," he said. "Let me try. Throw a punch."

I took aim at his chest and stepped forward with a *kihap*.

Bam!

Mark's forearm smashed into mine and sent my punch off course.

I tried a few more times. I even tried to fake him out once or twice. But with almost every punch, he got the block.

"You want to try again?" Mark asked.

I didn't really want to, but I nodded anyway.

Mark threw a few punches. Slower this time. I managed to kind of block one or two of them.

Hey! Maybe I was getting the hang of this.

The fourth punch was faster, though. Mark took a long step forward and threw his fist at my chest. I saw it coming and put my left arm up to block. But I knocked it up instead of away.

Ow-za!

My hand flew to my upper lip.

"Oh. Crud! I'm sorry!" Mark said when he realized he'd hit me. "Are you okay?"

"I think so," I told him. "Is it bleeding?"

I pulled my hand away, and he examined my face. "No. It's just red. I'm really sorry."

One of the black-belt helpers handed me one of those pop-and-shake ice packs. "Here. This'll keep the swelling down."

"I didn't mean to hit her," Mark said.

"It happens," the black belt told him. "Control is a tricky thing."

Then he turned to me. "Timing is a tricky thing, too. Don't worry. You'll get it."

The black belt walked away, and Mark kept apologizing. I told him about a dozen times it was okay.

Before Master Kim dismissed class, he had us sit down in our places.

"I'd like to give some advice about blocking," he said.

He wasn't looking my way, but I knew the advice was meant for me. I felt my cheeks get even warmer than they already were from class.

"Watch for little movements," Master Kim said. "Little movements give away bigger things to come."

It sounded like something you'd read in a fortune cookie. Great. I hated fortune cookies. They always crumbled.

After class Madison came up to me. "How's your lip?"

I shrugged. "Okay I guess."

"That's good," she said and then headed toward the door.

I couldn't tell if she was being serious or teasing me. She sounded like she was serious. Like she was trying to be nice. One minute she's not talking to me and scowling, and the next she's asking about my sore lip. What on planet Earth was *that* all about?

WHY I CHICKENED OUT OF ASKING FOR A NEW HANDBOOK

Mom had an early shift, so she was able to take me to taekwondo on Saturday afternoon. She still hadn't noticed I wasn't talking to her. But at least I didn't have to ride with Madison.

I was going to ask for a new handbook after class. I swear. But Master Kim was talking to Madison in the back of the room. And he wasn't smiling.

I'd noticed during class that Madison was standing in the back row. She wasn't wearing her belt, either.

I waited by the door and pretended my bag zipper was stuck. "A good martial artist is responsible for her own equipment," Master Kim told Madison. "If you forget your belt again, you will be asked to sit out class."

"Yes sir," she mumbled.

I kept fiddling with my bag, trying to come up with what I'd say, and missed Master Kim walking toward me.

"Did you need something, Eliza?"

My heart about jumped through my skin.

Words tumbled in my head like socks in a dryer. Handbook. Sweet Caroline. Ask. *Responsibility.*

"No sir," I told him.

I decided I'd just have to keep looking.

IN THE BATHROOM

When I went to change, Madison was in the bathroom, leaning over the sink and splashing water on her face. She looked up, and I caught her refection in the mirror. Her eyes were red and shiny.

I have no idea what possessed me—but I opened my big mouth. "I lose things all the time," I said. "I can't find my student handbook."

"I didn't *lose* my belt," she informed me with a sniff. "I forgot it."

"Oh."

"Yeah. Well," Madison said. She rubbed her nose a few times and then headed toward the door. "Okay."

"See ya Wednesday I guess," I called after her.

She was almost to the door and she wasn't facing me, but I thought I heard her say something back. And I could've sworn it sounded like, "See ya."

LIGHTS, CAMERA . . . OH

I had an orthodontist appointment on Tuesday. Dad drove Mom to work and then skipped his class so he could take me. He was going to have to do that for my Friday appointment, too.

The night before, I offered to bail on the whole braces thing if it was going to be so much trouble getting there; but Mom just said, "Nice try."

Dad and I were getting ready to leave when Sam came waltzing in. "Can I drive? I've got my ID." He flashed the wallet he'd bought over the weekend. The one with the see-through spot for his learner's license.

I scowled at him. "I don't want to ride with *you*. You run red lights."

"Just that once," Sam said like it was no big deal.

"Sure; why not?" Dad told him. "Why don't you grab the basketball, too? If we get done early, we can shoot some hoops over at the community center."

For once I hoped my orthodontist appointment ran long. Basketball, or more precisely, waiting on the hot bleachers *watching* basketball, was boring.

Unfortunately my appointment was just to get some spacers put in and have a mold taken. It didn't take that long. And the gooey mold stuff was supposed to taste like grape, but it didn't, so it wasn't turning out to be a good afternoon.

I balanced on the edge of the burning-hot metal bleachers and watched Dad and Sam join in a pickup game. I wished I had a book or nail polish or something. About twenty minutes into the game, Dad ran over and pulled out his wallet. "Here," he said, handing me a couple of dollar bills. "Go hit the vending machines. We'll be done soon, okay?" He was just in time. I was melting.

The cool air inside the community center froze the beads of sweat on my skin. It felt wonderful. *Ahhh* with a capital *A*. I bought a bag of cookies and a drink, and decided to walk around for a bit. Dad and Sam wouldn't miss me.

My feet ended up moving toward the cooking classroom. I hadn't seen it yet and just wanted to take a peek.

Instead of finding a deserted hallway, though, there was a commotion of sorts. Burly men with big stage lights and a skinny man pushing rolling cameras buzzed in and out of the room. A lady with a clipboard and a headset seemed to be directing everyone.

I moved slowly along the wall to where a guy who looked just a little older than Sam was leaning on a mop sticking out from one of those rolling buckets. "What's going on?" I asked him.

"Some TV cake lady is doing a show or sump'in," the guy said.

My heart did the cha-cha inside my chest. "Sweet Caroline is *here*?" I asked.

"Nah. I think she's coming tomorrow and doing her show during one of the classes," the guy answered. "They're just setting up now 'cuz the TV van had to be somewhere else. That's what I heard anyways."

Oh. My heart resumed normal speed.

But still. This was cool news. Tony was going to be on TV!

My first thought was that I had to call him. But my next thought was, *Why hadn't he called me?* Maybe he was afraid I'd be jealous. And, well okay, I was a little bit. But I was happy for him, too. Being on TV would look great on his résumé. Maybe it would help him get into a good pastry-chef school.

When I got home, I waited for the phone to ring for about an hour. Then I couldn't take it anymore and called Tony's house.

"He's not here," his sister said.

"Could you ask him to call Eliza please?" I asked.

"Sure. No problem."

"Thanks," I said before I hung up.

It was time to get things settled once and for all.

WEDNESDAY

Tony didn't call on Tuesday night or on Wednesday morning. Or Wednesday afternoon. I told myself he was just busy with the show, and he'd call later. The cake-decorating classroom was on the other side of the community center; but my stomach hurt (for real), so I stayed home from taekwondo anyway.

BIRTHDAY PARTIES AND OTHER THINGS THAT SHOULD BE AGAINST THE LAW

There wasn't a whole lot to do for the next couple of days. Mom was working, Dad was studying; Sam was playing on the computer, and certain other people were busy not calling me back. I was so bored that I *almost* looked forward to going to the orthodontist.

Dad checked his watch as the two of us sat in the waiting room. "Dr. Ohno must be running behind."

Ohno.

That cracked me up every time. Get it? It's like "*Oh no!* The orthodontist is coming! Run! Hide!"

I didn't care if the doctor was running late. It wasn't like I was looking forward to getting my braces. Plus it gave me more time to reread my favorite book, *Savvy* by Ingrid Law. It was about a girl named Mibs who got special powers on her thirteenth birthday. I wished I had special powers. Or at the very least, straight teeth.

Unfortunately Dr. Ohno's assistant eventually showed up and took me back. Two long and boring hours later, I was standing in front of the mirror in the hallway. I checked out my new braces and the purple bands I'd picked out. Gently rubbing my jaw, I decided making someone keep their mouth open for two hours should be against the law. So should nasty-tasting-bracket glue. And pokey wires, too, for that matter.

"Hi Eliza!" someone said.

I turned to see a girl walking toward me. Her name was Annie, and she was in my class at school. I waved.

Annie talked faster than anyone I knew. Especially when she was excited. She also talked *a lot*. But she was one of the few people who was nice to me.

"I'msogladIranintoyou!" she said. "I was gonna call, but now I don't have to. You're coming to Tony's birthday party next week, right? Duh! Of course you are! I just got him a gift card. It's not that exciting but I don't know what guys like. Aren't you stoked about getting to go to his parents' bakery? Tony says we're going to decorate our own individual cakes. Won't that be awesome? I can't wait. Well, my moms are waiting for me. The three of us are going to a movie and then dinner. See ya!"

I stared after her as she bounced down the hallway and out the door that led to the waiting area. I didn't dare move. I was too afraid that if I did, the tears in my eyes would spill over.

I WASN'T INVITED

I managed to keep a poker face the whole way home. But when I got there, I headed straight upstairs. My eyes started prickling again even before I got to my room.

I opened my closet door and stared at my to-do list: *4. Decide what to get Tony for his birthday party.*

I guess Tony had decided for me, so I got a pencil and crossed it off.

I stared at the piece of paper and rubbed my wet cheeks with the back of my hand. Stupid tears. Stupid Tony!

I imagined him with a stack of invitations. Maybe his mom said, "What about that lovely girl Eliza? The one who helped us with the cupcakes that one day. Aren't you going to invite her?" And Tony lying, "Nah. She moved away."

I thought about how all the kids would show up, including Annie, and how everyone would get to make their own cakes and sing "Happy Birthday" and . . . and. . . .

A sob snuck up on me and made it hard to breathe. The more I tried to fight back the tears, the harder and faster they came. After a while, I just gave in, sat down on my bedroom floor, and bawled my eyes out.

When I was done, my head ached, and my arms and legs felt like they weighed a thousand pounds each. I climbed into bed and even though it was the afternoon, I pulled the covers over my head. I must have fallen asleep because the next thing I knew, Mom was knocking on my door.

"Can I come in?" she asked.

"It's open," I croaked and then rubbed my puffy eyes.

Mom came in and put an ibuprofen tablet and a glass of water on my nightstand.

"How you doing, sweetie?" she asked, settling on the edge of my bed. "Let's see your braces."

I sat up and showed her my mouth full of metal.

"Nice. I like the purple bands," Mom said. "How do they feel?"

I had a sudden urge to hug my mom, so I wrapped my arms around her neck.

"Poor Eliza," she said, patting my back. "Your mouth hurts a lot, huh?"

It wasn't my mouth that hurt, but the truth was stuck in my throat.

"It's okay," Mom told me in a soothing voice. "Everything will be okay."

I nodded and let her hug me tighter.

1. ~~KEEP GIVING MOM THE SILENT TREATMENT UNTIL SHE NOTICES I'M NOT TALKING TO HER.~~

KER-POW!

Saturday was hot with a capital H.

I got so desperate that I dragged out the sprinkler. After about twenty minutes, I got bored. My legs were all muddy and grassy, too. I did my best to rinse off with the hose and then laid my towel out on the driveway.

I had a couple of hours till taekwondo class. It didn't look like Tony and I would be opening a shop together after all, but I still wanted to take Sweet Caroline's class.

And that meant I had to finish taekwondo. Besides, there were only a few weeks left before the belt test.

The concrete was burning, but I was seeing how much longer I could stand to lie on it when Dad pulled in.

"You made a mud patch," he said as he opened the trunk of Mom's car. He didn't sound happy. "And did you make sure to turn off the hose? Water costs money."

I sat up. "Sorry."

I helped Dad bring in the groceries. He'd bought store-brand chips. When I complained, he scowled. "I forgot my coupons."

At least Master Kim was in a better mood than Dad. There was excitement in his voice when told us he'd brought something new for us to try out during class: a shield.

I wondered if we'd get cool rubber weapons to use, too. Turned out the shield wasn't a metal shield like a knight would use to block a sword attack. It was just this thing that sort of looked like a hard rectangular pillow. Master Kim went around the classroom, holding the shield for each person to do a few back kicks. While we waited for our turn, we were supposed to practice.

I managed to avoid being Madison's partner and ended up with some boy who didn't talk. He was taller than me and held the kicking paddle too high. I kept kicking the edge and sliding off or missing it altogether.

I noticed a couple of my toes had chipped polish. That made me think of that first time I saw Madison, and only half of her toes were painted. I couldn't help it. I peeked over at her. Madison was throwing perfect back kicks. Well, at least prettier than mine.

"Eliza."

It was Master Kim. He was standing next to me, but I had no idea when he'd shown up.

I swallowed. "Yes sir?"

"You're not following through."

"No sir," I said. "I mean, okay sir."

"You seem a bit distracted today," he said sternly. "Your training is suffering."

"Yes sir."

Master Kim lowered the shield and looked right at me. "A good martial artist does his or her best at all times."

"Yes sir," I said with a quick bow.

Master Kim stood sideways in front of me and held the shield against his side. "Now throw your kick," he said. "Don't think: Just do it. The Japanese call it *mushin*, or having no mind."

I didn't understand how someone could *not* think, but I took a deep breath and tried kicking the shield. My foot went too low.

"Again," Master Kim told me calmly.

I started my next kick too far away so my leg was almost straight when my heel landed. No power.

"Again," Master Kim said, still calm.

I lost balance while pivoting on the next try and had to stop midkick to keep myself from wobbling over.

Master Kim remained steady. "Again," he said. "And *kihap*."

Again, again, again. It was driving me crazy. What did he want from me? I couldn't think straight. And I couldn't do the kick!

I couldn't do *anything*. I couldn't magically give Dad money. I couldn't see Mom as much as I wanted. I couldn't stop school from starting. Shoot. I couldn't even get invited to my own friend's birthday party!

"Don't think," Master Kim said.

I looked at him, and he gave me a nod.

"Don't think," he said again. "Just kick."

I closed my eyes and concentrated on the hum of the lights and my breathing. In. Out. In. Out. Just kick.

Okay. I thought, *That's something I can do.*

I opened my eyes, stepped back into my fighting stance, and stared at the shield. Then I pivoted, looked over my shoulder, pulled my leg in tight, and shot it straight back. I imagined all my power traveling through my hip, down my leg, and into my foot. At the same time, I yelled, "Hup!"

My heel landed smack in the middle of the shield. And it landed hard. *Whumph!*

Master Kim smiled. It wasn't a big smile, but it was there. "Good," he said.

My chest was pounding and I couldn't help grinning. *Did I just do that?*

That felt so great. It was like I was superhero! Like I could do anything! Like I could break a board or jump over a car or kick a door down and save someone from a burning building.

QUIZ TIME

On Wednesday, Madison was sitting in the front seat of the car again so I climbed into the back. It felt strange being there alone. Kind of like I was in a taxi or something. I had to bite the inside of my cheek not to say, "To taekwondo. And step on it!"

Cookie called me sweetheart and asked me how my week went. But then she took a sip from her coffee and said, "Great," even though I hadn't answered her yet.

"Hey," Madison said in my direction as way of a greeting. She went back to reading whatever was in her lap.

I watched out the window and counted seven drivers talking on their cell phones before I got bored. I started wondering what Madison was reading that was so interesting.

I scootched over and gently tugged on my shoulder strap to get some wiggle room. Then I stretched my neck just a bit.

Madison caught me looking. "Studying for my belt test," she said as she held up her student handbook. "I'm going for my green belt next. If I pass, then I can move up to the intermediate class and go to the *dojang* that Master Kim's dad owns."

Cookie let out a huge sigh. And I noticed Madison's happy expression faded a bit.

I felt bad for her. "I could quiz you if you want," I blurted out.

Madison passed the folder over the seat and gave me a half smile.

I went through her test requirements a few times and quizzed her on old stuff as well. I couldn't believe how many Korean words and definitions she had to know. Madison had to know *four* forms, too.

"What are the five tenets of taekwondo?" I asked her.

She began counting them off on her fingers. "Courtesy. Integrity. Perseverance. Self-control, and indomitable spirit."

I gave her a thumbs-up.

Madison grinned.

Cookie sighed loudly again.

Madison's grin fell. "That's good. Thanks," she told me and then twisted in her seat so she was facing forward.

We were almost to the community center. I suddenly realized that I hadn't given back the handbook. Cool beans! As quietly as I could, I flipped back to the page where *my* test requirements were listed:

Break a board using push kick. *All right. Got it.*

Counting to ten. Knew that one.

Kicho il bo. I knew that, too.

Wrist escape. Cripes. That needed work.

And all those names of techniques and commands in Korean? *Ahnjoe, koomahn, ap chagi, yursit*—the list went on and on. I forgot what half of them meant. I tried not to panic.

The definition of *taekwondo. Yikes!* I read as quickly as I could. "Taekwondo . . . Korean art . . . hand and foot—"

"We're here!" Cookie sang out.

My head snapped up. Madison was looking at me like she was confused about something. I shut the handbook and gave it back to her.

"Madison," Cookie said. "Don't forget. Your father is expecting you later tonight so no dillydallying after class."

Something about the way Cookie said the word *father* made me realize Madison's parents were divorced. And it made me feel sorry for her all over again.

ALL WET

For once Mom had a day off on the same day Dad did. *And* we'd finally gotten his car back from the mechanic. We celebrated by hitting the pool on Friday. It wasn't exactly the whole-day-alone-with-Mom thing I wanted, but it was close enough.

It was a million degrees, and the pool was packed. Sam

threw down his stuff and ran off to join friends. I spread my towel on the grassy patch Mom and Dad found.

"There's a ton of kids here this afternoon," Mom said, laying her towel between me and Dad. "Anyone you know?"

Earlier in the week, she'd been oh-so-casually asking about kids from school and suggesting I call someone to see if they wanted to come with me to the new student orientation. I'd thought about calling Annie, but that would mean having to explain why I wasn't at Tony's party.

"Nope," I told Mom.

I lay down, threw an arm over my eyes, and practiced *kicho il bo* in my head. I made it through about three times before I started wondering if armpits could get sunburned.

"Can you help me out here, hon?" I heard my dad say.

Peeking under my arm, I saw my mom slathering sunscreen on my dad's back.

June's moon.

I mumbled something about being hot and booked it out of there before they could start making googly eyes at each other.

I cannonballed off the diving board. When I came up, I went under the deep-end rope and leaned against the pool wall in the shallower end. Sam was playing water basketball with a bunch of guys at the opposite end of the pool. I scanned the rest of the place.

And that's when I noticed them.

Madison and a group of about eight girls were spread

out on a large quilt near the back fence. I recognized most of them from school. They were the ones who wore matching CHEER CAMP T-shirts the last week of fifth grade. They were all laughing, passing around bags of Cheetos, and poking each other with orange fingers. Madison shrieked when someone reached for her shoulder and then laughed even harder.

I dunked under and swam along the bottom of the pool until my lungs felt like they were going to burst. When I came up, the stinging in my eyes wasn't just from the chlorine.

I wasn't in the mood to swim anymore, so I headed back to get my towel. Mom grabbed her wallet when she saw me. "Here," she said, handing me a five. "Will you go get me a bottled water? You can get yourself something, too."

"Sure," I told her. I had nothing else to do.

I decided on a raspberry Sno-Cone. (Why is raspberry flavor blue? Shouldn't it be red?) I was trying to balance the Sno-Cone in one hand and Mom's water and the change I'd gotten back in the other hand, when the speaker crackled on. It was time for the hourly break. Everyone but grown-ups had to clear the pool. Suddenly the deck filled with dripping, shivering kids, and there was a mad dash for the concession stand.

I took the long way around to try and avoid the stampede, but that meant walking near Madison and her friends.

My plan was to keep my head down and pretend to be concentrating on not dropping anything. But I accidentally peeked as I went by.

Madison caught my eye. She put her hand up. She didn't move it or anything, but I knew it was a hello. I gave what I hoped was a friendly nod and kept on moving. It took me a few seconds to remember to exhale.

THE BIG "NO BIG DEAL"

After class on Saturday, Madison called me over. When I got to her, she leaned over and pulled something out of her bag. "I brought something for you," she said, handing me a folder.

I looked down at what she'd put in my hand. It was a taekwondo handbook.

"Th-thanks," I managed.

"No big deal. You needed one."

"How did you get it?"

Madison got a mischievous grin. "I used my mom's copier. She's a realtor so she has one in her office at home. I'm not supposed to be in there, but . . ." She shrugged.

"Won't you get in trouble?"

Madison grabbed her stuff off the floor and headed toward the door. "Not now," she said over her shoulder. "She didn't catch me."

COUNTDOWN: FOURTEEN DAYS

The first thing I did when I got home was clear off everything and put the handbook on top of my desk. Smack in the middle.

The second thing I did was to make a paper chain. I had exactly fourteen days until the belt test, so I made a chain with thirteen white links and one yellow one. Master Kim told us to visualize our goals. The yellow was in honor of my new belt color.

I hung the paper chain on my bulletin board. And then I sat at my desk, opened the handbook, and made twenty flash cards with all the words and phrases I had to know.

The flash cards were yellow, too.

SWEET CAROLINE WOULD UNDERSTAND

By lunchtime on Monday, I had memorized about half of the flash cards. There were some I still couldn't pronounce. Like the words for riding-horse stance with a punch: *juchum-seogi jireugi*. In my head, I could hear it, but I just couldn't get my mouth to make the right sounds. I hoped Master Kim would count it right if we got close enough.

I needed to practice my push kick. I got only three tries to break the board at my test. If I couldn't break it, I failed. Too bad, so sad. Try again in another three months. Dad and I drove by a garage sale on our way to the grocery store, but we didn't see any kicking bags. Just treadmills and stationary bikes.

I went to our basement and climbed into the crawl space to look for something I could use to make my own bag. I found the pile of boxes with GIVE AWAY scrawled on the sides. It was mostly clothes, but I hoped there might be something useful.

And . . . bingo!

In the third box, I found Sam's old comforter. It still had plenty of puffiness. I dragged it out of the dusty crawl space and shook it in case any spiders had taken up residence. All folded up tight, it made a good-size rectangle. I got the duct tape off Dad's workbench. It took me half an hour to wrap the blanket up. When it was done, it looked just a little smaller than the kicking shields Master Kim brought to class.

I tore off another strip of duct tape, folded it in half lengthwise, and attached it to the top of the shield to create a handle. One end of a rope tied to the handle and the other end tied to one of the basement rafters and ta-da! My very own kicking bag.

I got into fighting stance and threw a push kick. My homemade bag went flying. It was hard to tell if I was standing the right distance away and if I had the right amount of strength to actually break a board. But Master Kim said successful board breaks were more about getting the right technique than having a lot of strength. I hoped he was right. Plus, at test time, someone would be holding my board and so it wouldn't give as much. I stopped the bag from swinging and kept practicing.

Bear came downstairs. She cocked her head and whined the way she does when she needs to go out.

"Okay, girl," I told her. "I could use a break anyway."

When the two of us got upstairs, Sam was in the kitchen, warming something in the microwave. "Where've you been?" he asked.

"Practicing," I said.

"I thought you called the TV all day. If you're not going to watch it, I'm going to."

Crispy fried eggs!

I'd completely forgotten that *Sweet Caroline Cakes* was the Monday marathon on channel thirteen.

Oh well. Sweet Caroline would just have to understand.

TEN DAYS AND COUNTING

I think every student showed up for taekwondo class.

"I've never seen it so crowded," I said to Mark.

"This always happens right before a test," he said. "Everyone tries to get in all the last-minute practice they can."

Master Kim seemed to be trying to get in all the last-minute teaching he could, too.

We ran through the basic motions. The only ones I mixed up were front kick and side kick. *Ap chagi* and *yup chagi*. They sounded so much alike! *Okay*, I thought. *Ap sounds like op and that's short for operation and when SWAT teams do sting operations they* kick *open* front *doors. And when one of the SWAT guys asks the captain if he needs help, the captain says,* "Yup, go kick *in the* side *door."*

Next we paired up and practiced escapes. I tried to move the second I felt Rosa grab my arm (like the black belt told me), but I still could escape only about half of the time. I'd have to keep working on that.

I got a chance to practice my push kick on a real kicking

paddle. That went better than my escape. I nailed it every time. Pulled my leg in tightly, snapped out my foot, and *pow*!

The last thing we practiced was forms. And a strange thing happened.

I was standing in my row. Master Kim called out, "*Choonbi.*" As I moved into the ready position, I could feel my heart pick up speed. My brain clicked off, like a television, and all I got was a blank screen. Oh man. What was the first move of *kicho il bo*?

Think. Think. Think.

Master Kim looked around the room slowly. "*Shijak!*" Begin.

My brain stayed locked but—Holy Toledo!—my arms and legs moved on their own.

Lower block. Punch. Punch. Punch. "Hup!"

I was doing it!

I just kept moving, trusting my arms and legs to go where they were supposed to. It was kind of like this one time my grandparents took me to the water park, and I got swept up in the wave pool. But in a good way.

Before I knew it, I was done with my form. And hadn't missed a single block, punch, or *kihap*.

Afterward I sat down against the wall to watch the other students go through their forms. My cheeks hurt from grinning so hard.

Maybe *that's* what Master Kim had meant when he talked about doing something with no mind.

AT THE END OF CLASS I TURNED IN MY APPLICATION

A re you ready?" Dad asked when I met him in the hall.

"I'm ready," I told him.

And it was the truth.

MESSES

O n Friday my pill and water weren't on the counter. That happened sometimes when Mom was running late for her shift. I'd have to remember to ask Dad to get it for me when he came in from pulling weeds. I couldn't miss it. That afternoon was sixth-grade orientation, and I wanted to make a good impression.

I toasted a couple of Wild! Berry Pop-Tarts and plopped down at the computer. I flipped on the TV in the background while I played *Penny's Pet Groomer* on the computer. Since I already had a gazillion good-groomer stars, I got a little crazy. I started giving the dogs orange mohawks and shaved smiley faces into the cats. I liked when the customers came into the virtual shop with speech bubbles of pretend cursing over their heads.

Right after the first four contestants on *The Price Is Right* were told to "Come on down!" Dad popped in, filled his water bottle, and grabbed his keys.

"I'll be right back. I gotta get some gas for the lawn mower," he said. "Think you can stay out of trouble for a while?"

"Do monkeys have tails?" I asked.

Dad grinned. "That's my girl!"

I quit my game, grabbed the remote, and surfed through about a hundred stations. Nothing looked all that interesting. I decided to paint my nails. Each one a different color.

Sam came down in the middle of me trying to clean up the nail-polish remover I accidentally knocked over on the kitchen floor. He shook his head and laughed. "You're gonna be in so much trouble."

He was right. I was supposed to put down newspaper if I painted my nails on the wood floor. I scowled as hard as I could at him. "Go away."

"Whatever," Sam said as he headed down the hall.

It took seven paper towels, but the floor didn't look too bad when I was done. Of course, then I had another problem. The paper towels stunk from here to next year. If I threw them away in the trash can, Mom was going to notice. And then she'd know I'd broken the rules.

Dad was going to be home any second, too. I wadded up all the evidence and headed for the bathroom. In a movie once, I'd seen a bad guy flush some incriminating papers down the toilet, so I threw in the towels and pushed the handle.

The paper towels were all going down! Yes! It had worked!

But then, ever so slowly, the water began rising. And rising. And rising.

Stop, I begged. *Please stop.*

But the water kept right on rising and began spilling over the edge of the toilet and onto the floor.

I thought I heard the garage door opening. Oh no. Dad was home!

I ran up the stairs, taking them two at a time, yanked open the linen closet, and grabbed some bath towels.

I came back down as quickly as I could, but I wasn't going to be fast enough. Desperate times call for desperate measures so I jumped the last five stairs. When I landed, my feet slipped out from underneath me.

I sat down.

Hard.

A sharp pain traveled up my spine and rattled my teeth. I wanted to call for help, but I couldn't breathe.

WHAT HURTS?

The *thud* got Sam's attention. "Eliza?" he called. When I didn't answer, he came looking for me.

I heard his footsteps in the living room and then in the kitchen. I opened my mouth, but I still couldn't breathe. Tears stung my eyes. It seemed like forever until he found me.

At first he was smirking, but then he saw me sitting on the floor at the bottom of the stairs with my legs straight out in front of me.

Sam knelt down and put a hand gently on my shoulder. "E, what happened?" he asked.

I tried inhaling again and this time, thankfully, I managed to squeeze some air into my lungs.

"Fell," I told him.

"Down the stairs?" The color drained from Sam's face. "Is anything broken?"

I didn't like the panic in his voice and now that I had my breath back, I started to cry for real.

Sam squeezed my shoulder. "It's okay. You're okay," he said. "Just tell me what hurts."

I swallowed a sob. Only one thing really, really hurt.

"Don't laugh," I told him.

"I won't laugh," Sam said. "I swear."

"My butt."

Sam got a funny look on his face, but he didn't laugh. "Should I call nine-one-one?"

I shook my head. I wanted Mom, but she was at work. "Get Dad," I said.

But it turned out Dad wasn't home yet. I'd only heard a truck rumbling by. Sam pulled out his cell phone and dialed. Dad insisted on talking to me himself.

"Are you okay?" he asked. He voice was tight.

"Yes," I told him. "But can you please come home?"

"I'm already on my way."

After I hung up and handed the phone back to Sam, I started crying again. "I need to blow my nose," I said.

"I'll get you some toilet paper."

Sam came back a few seconds later. "Boy," he said with a tiny tease in his voice. "You sure made a mess."

He was right.

AT THE ER

My dad's a Nervous Nelly when it comes to me or Sam getting hurt. This is why I ended up in one of the exam rooms of Mom's ER, holding an ice pack against my backside. Dad kept asking me if I wanted to get on the gurney, but the last thing I wanted to do was sit. On the drive over, Dad let me break the seat-belt rule and lie across the backseat of the Jeep.

"You're going to be fine," Mom told me as she stroked my hair. "I think you bruised your tailbone."

"Is that bad?" I asked.

"Mostly just uncomfortable," Mom said. "But since you're already here, we're going to have one of the emergency-room physicians take a look."

It was so embarrassing. Beyond embarrassing. (Thank the stars Mom suggested Dad step out of the room and go call Sam.) The doctor had to pull down my shorts a bit, and then she pressed her fingers around the bottom of my spine. Which, is, well, you know where it is. And even though Mom had given me some ibuprofen when I first arrived, I squeezed her hand the whole time to fight the pain. She kept reminding me to breathe.

Then I had to get X rays.

Of. My. Butt!

There was pain when I walked. Pain when I sat down. And my stomach was growling since it was a couple of hours past lunchtime. Mom snuck down to the nurses' lounge and swiped a slice of pizza for me. Dad went to the vending machine and got some pop and a couple of bags of chips. When he came back, he looked at me seriously. "I'm so sorry," he said. "I just realized I forgot to put your pill out this morning."

"It's okay," I told him. "I could have asked Sam. So it's kind of my fault, too."

I suddenly remembered something. "Oh no!" I said.

"What is it, honey?" Mom asked.

"I'm missing orientation!"

"Oh, don't worry about that," Dad said. "I'm sure we

can pick up your schedule and get your locker combination later."

"Are you sure?"

"Positive," Dad said.

"Positive," Mom agreed, wrapping her arm around me.

The three of us went back to our weird, everyone-standing picnic. Just as we finished up, the doctor came back in. "Well, good news," she said. "No fracture or dislocation. It's a slight contusion of the coccyx."

Mom's shoulders relaxed. "See, I told you."

A contusion? Of the what? Those sounded serious.

I must have looked confused because Dad said, "Your coccyx is your tailbone."

"A contusion is the fancy name for a bruise," the doctor said to me as she handed Mom a prescription for pain medicine. "Rest and ice, and you'll be good as new in a week or two."

I grabbed Mom's arm in a panic. "But my belt test is in *eight days.*"

"Let's not worry about that just now," Dad said.

"Honey, all I'm concerned about is getting you home and spoiling you rotten," Mom said. "We'll talk about it later."

I suddenly felt too tired to argue.

The doctor left and a few minutes later, a nurse came back with an inflated thing that looked like a miniature life preserver. Mom called it a donut and said it was for sitting on.

"Cool," Dad said. "It's a sweet-cheek seat! Get it? Huh?"

"Or a tooshie cushie," I said, getting into the spirit.

Dad and I looked at Mom, waiting to see what she'd say.

"You two are incorrigible," she said. But then a devilish grin spread across her face. "I sure hope all these bun puns are done!"

MY BROTHER THE COMEDIAN

Mom got the rest of the day off. She helped me get set up on the couch with a DVD and then went to make chocolate-chip cookies. Dad went to the pharmacy.

A little ways into the movie, Sam came in the living room and slumped in the easy chair. "I cleaned up the bathroom for you," he said.

"Thanks."

He shrugged. "Whatever."

He watched the movie for a minute or two and then stood up to go. "Anyway. I'm glad you're not paralyzed or anything."

"Thanks. I guess."

"Hey, at least now you know how I feel when you're around," he said.

"Whadda ya mean?"

"You know," he said with a crooked grin. "You got a pain in your butt."

That made us both crack up.

TANGLED

It took forever to climb the stairs at bedtime because I had to go one foot up, rest, other foot up, rest. Mom and Dad said I could sleep downstairs on the couch if I wanted, but I wanted to sleep in my own bed.

"Been a long day, huh?" Mom said as she helped me with my covers.

"You can say that again."

"You're going to feel so much better tomorrow. I promise."

Mom flipped on my night-light and sat on the edge of my mattress to lightly rub circles on my back. It felt so good, like my body was floating. Now that I was lying on my stomach, my tailbone didn't hurt as much. The day drained away.

"I'll have Dad call Master Kim tomorrow," Mom said. "And let him know you're done with class."

My eyes popped open.

I rolled up on my side. "I can't miss the test," I told her.

"Honey, you're hurt. Master Kim will understand."

My thoughts were all tangled up. Now that I *couldn't* take the test, I felt . . . what did I feel?

"But I *have* to take the test."

Mom's eyes narrowed. "Is this about the cake-decorating class? Don't worry about that. You held up your end of the bargain and stuck with taekwondo. I'm proud of you. It isn't your fault you can't take the test. You can still take the fall cake class, okay?"

I rolled back on my stomach, and Mom started rubbing circles again. My thoughts were even more tangled.

I could take the cake-decorating class. It was what I'd been working for. It was what I'd wanted all along. That was great news. Wasn't it?

The only thing was, I kept thinking about Flying Ninja Girl and Madison and my crisp, white *dobok* hanging in the laundry room. And how I'd finally done *kicho il bo* without having to think, and how good it felt when I'd figured out how to do a wrist escape and landed that back kick. I thought about my flash cards and how many times I practiced my push kick and how I'd been looking forward to breaking a board.

I thought about Master Kim tying a yellow belt around my waist.

I couldn't believe that wasn't going to happen. All because I did something stupid.

My days as a martial artist were over.

And I felt . . .

I felt sad.

THE PART WHERE I NEGOTIATE ANOTHER DEAL

As Mom headed to my bedroom door, I called out to her. "What do you need, honey?"

"Can you not call Master Kim just yet?" I asked. "I mean, maybe I can still take the test."

"But Eliza . . ."

"Can't we wait and see how I feel? Please?"

Mom frowned. "I don't want you to push yourself. A bruised coccyx is nothing to mess with."

"If I take it easy and keep the ice on for the rest of the week?"

"Eliza Nicole Bing resting for a *whole week?*" Mom teased.

I ignored her. "But what if I do? Then can I?"

"We'll see," Mom said. "Now get some sleep."

We'll see.

At least there was hope.

THE COOL THING
THAT HAPPENED THE
NEXT MORNING

The next morning, Sam told me I had a message on the answering machine.

"I would have told you sooner," he said. "But I forgot. Sorry."

"Who was it?" I asked him.

"I can't remember. I only heard the first part, and it was kind of confusing. Go listen yourself."

I wobbled to the kitchen and saw the blinking light. It had to be Tony. Right? Who else would it be?

I pressed the PLAY button.

"Hey, Eliza. This is Annie." (Only it came out as, "HeyElizathisisAnnie.")

She went on. "I didn't see you at orientation today. I was wondering who you got for homeroom. I got Ms. Naylor. Maybe you did, too. I hope so. Anyway, call me back when you get a chance. Or I guess I'll see you on the first day of school. Man, I can't believe summer is almost over. That stinks. Well, um. Okay. Bye. And oh, I can't remember if I said it or not, in case I didn't, this is Annie. Bye."

The machine beeped to let me know the message had ended. I stared at the light, which wasn't blinking anymore.

I tried to decide if I should erase the message or keep it. I played it one more time. Just to make sure I'd heard it right.

Huh. Annie looked for me. *And* she'd called me.

I was surprised and shocked. Kind of like that day I got hit in the lip at taekwondo. The day Master Kim said to watch out for small movements because they gave away hints of bigger things to come.

FRIENDS?

Annie had never called me before. It was kind of a miracle, actually. And I started wondering if one miracle could turn into two, so I picked up the phone.

I called Tony at the bakery. I'm glad the person who answered didn't ask who was calling because I think I would have chickened out if I had to give my name.

"Oh, hey. What's up?" Tony said after I said hello. He didn't sound excited.

"Hi." I bit my lip. "I just wanted to wish you a happy late birthday."

He didn't say anything right away. Maybe he thought I was trying to make him feel bad about not inviting me to his party. But that wasn't it. Despite everything, he was my friend. I really meant it about wishing him a happy birthday.

"Thanks," Tony finally said. There was another long pause. "I would've invited you, but I didn't think you wanted to come."

"Why?" I asked.

"Because at the mall you acted all mad at me or something," Tony said.

For the second time in an hour, I was shocked. "I wasn't mad," I explained. "I was just trying not to embarrass you in front of that Kevin guy."

"Well, that's how it seemed," Tony said.

"I'm sorry," I said. "I guess I messed up."

Tony was quiet. But I could hear people in the bakery in the background. I wondered if the cranky cake decorator was nearby, glaring at him.

"I'm sorry, too," Tony said. "Look, I can't talk now. The bakery is super busy."

I wasn't ready to let him go. But I didn't really have a choice. "Okay," I said. "Friends?"

I held my breath.

"Sure," Tony said brightly.

But I could tell he was just being nice.

Maybe he was just being nice all along.

MOXIE

I'd spent almost three days carrying around my inflatable donut and icing my tailbone until it was numb, but Dad still wanted to call Master Kim and tell him I wouldn't be in class.

"I'm fine," I told him, walking across the room to show him how I could do it without wincing.

"What about kicking, though?"

I pulled my leg up to do a push kick in the air.

Even though I tried to keep a poker face, Dad said, "You're grimacing."

"It's not that bad," I protested. "Besides, a good martial artist pushes through pain." Master Kim never actually said that, but I thought it sounded good.

"Mom and I admire your moxie," Dad told me. "But a belt test isn't more important than your health."

I went back to the couch with my ice and another ibuprofen while Dad picked up the phone.

I didn't want moxie or anyone's admiration. I wanted my yellow belt.

TORTURE

I took it easy for the rest of the week. I memorized all of my flash cards and visualized the basic motions, my form and wrist escape and board break so many times that I could do them in my sleep.

I wondered if it was possible to go crazy from sitting on a couch.

TEST DAY

Saturday.

Test day.

I woke up with a queasy feeling, but I got out of bed and brushed my teeth. It was only six-thirty, and no one else was awake. When school started again in four days, everyone would be getting up that early. (The thought of school made me even queasier.)

I crept downstairs. I felt a little stiff, but my tailbone didn't hurt too much. Bear got up off her rug and whined, so I opened the back door. I followed her out to the yard.

The wet grass was cool against my feet. It was quiet, and the air smelled new, like the night had scrubbed everything clean. I turned and closed my eyes. The sun warmed my face, and I took a deep breath and held it as long as I could. My queasy feeling went away.

Bear began to bark, and I opened my eyes to find her sitting in front of me.

"Sorry, girl," I said, laughing. "Didn't mean to freak you out."

Bear stayed planted.

"Go play, you silly dog. You've got this whole big yard."

Hmm. Big yard . . . I had plenty of space. And no one was looking except Bear.

I inhaled slowly and lowered my hands into ready position. Then I did *kicho il bo*. It was the first time I'd done it for real (not in my head) in almost a week. I moved slowly, thinking about the wet grass and my tender tailbone.

It wasn't as powerful as normal, but I did it.

"Hey, girl!" I said to Bear. "Did you see that?"

Bear barked and ran after a bird. While she played, I tried out a few more moves. I could block and punch and kick. I even tried my push kick. My tailbone didn't hurt too much as long as I was careful.

Bear and I stayed out a bit longer and played catch with an old tennis ball. When we finally went back inside, I was surprised to see Dad standing in the kitchen, arranging vitamin bottles on the sink windowsill.

"Give me a second, and I'll get your medicine," he said when he saw me.

"Okay."

I leaned against the table and waited as Dad poured himself coffee. I tried to come up with the perfect way to convince him my tailbone was healed enough for me to take the test.

The weird thing was, it didn't take much convincing.

"Today's the big day, huh?" Dad asked. "Do you think you're up for it?"

"Yes," I said.

Dad studied me for a moment. "Alrighty then. I'd better make you a good breakfast. How about pancakes?"

"Dad's making pancakes?" Mom said, walking in. "What's the occasion?"

"Test day," I told her.

Mom put her hands on her hips, looked at Dad, and then back at me.

"I thought we settled this," she said. "You can't test with a bruised tailbone."

"But it's okay now," I told her. "It doesn't hurt that much."

"Eliza, sweetie . . ." Mom started.

"I want to, Mom."

Dad handed Mom a cup of coffee. "She's worked hard. What's the harm in letting her try?" he asked her. "If she thinks she's up for it, maybe we should trust her."

Mom moved to the fridge to grab some milk for her coffee. "So apparently I'm being ganged up on here." She was trying to sound like she was joking, but I could tell she was unhappy.

"Honey," Dad told her gently, "she's kept her end of the bargain."

Mom knitted her eyebrows and looked at me.

"I promise I'll stop if it hurts," I told her. "But I need to try. If I don't, I'll always wonder if I could've done it."

Mom walked across the kitchen, and put her arm around my shoulders. "Man, you're getting mature," she said. "And tall! When did that happen?"

"I don't know. When you weren't paying attention?"

I meant it as a joke, but Mom's eyes got all teary.

"Fine," she said, pulling out a smile. "I guess it's pancakes all around for test day."

CHOONBI
(READY POSITION)

The queasy feeling returned as I got in line with all the other taekwondo students. Madison explained that we were supposed to sign in before the test.

"No offense, but you look a little green," she said.

I shrugged, hoping my pancakes stayed where they were.

"It's probably nerves," Madison said. "It'll be fine once we start."

"Are you nervous?" I asked.

"Yeah. A little," she said as she tightened her belt for the third time. "I really want to move up to the intermediate class."

The lined moved quickly. "Your turn," Madison said after she'd signed in.

I picked up the pencil on the table, leaned over the sign-up sheet, and scribbled my name, just wanting to get the whole test thing started. I was about to hand the pencil to the kid behind me when something caught my eye.

Madison's name. Right above mine. Instead of large, loopy letters, it was in tiny, tight little letters. And there were no swirls above her *i*'s.

My heart jumped into my throat.

Maybe she'd changed her handwriting since she wrote the Every Day Eliza note. That was possible, right? Maybe she'd decided to go with a more mature signature since we were going into middle school. Or maybe she only dotted her *i*'s in a swirly way when she was with her friends. Or on mean notes.

But none of that made any sense.

I snapped my head up and looked at Madison, who by that time was busy talking to someone else. It was like a strange, time-travel thing—as if Past Me had known her for a long time but Here-and-Now Me was just meeting her for the first time. And right then I knew. I don't know how, but I knew deep in my bones. She hadn't changed her handwriting; she'd told the truth about the note last year. She *hadn't* been the one who'd given me the nickname. I'd been wrong all this time. Why hadn't I seen that before?

And if I'd been wrong about Madison, what else had I been wrong about?

What if I was wrong about being ready for the test?

JUDGES AND JELLY LEGS

Parents were allowed to watch the test, and I saw Mom wave from her spot along the wall. Dad fiddled with his camera. I was happy Mom traded shifts with someone at the last minute, but having them both there made me more nervous.

"Hey, where's your mom?" I asked Madison.

"She doesn't come to tests. My dad brought me. He's over there," she said pointing. "He's the one who pays for all my classes and gear anyway. He used to take taekwondo, too. When he was a teenager."

"Oh," I said. That's all I could come up with. I was too nervous and still trying to wrap my brain around what I'd found out about Madison and the note. I suspected that was going to take a while. But I didn't have time right then and there. I had to focus on the test.

I looked around at the other students. Some were standing like Madison and me. Others were running in place or practicing their forms.

I tried to avoid looking at the front of the room. I'd made *that* mistake when I first came in. There was a long table there. The table was covered with a black cloth, which had a bunch of gold Korean writing on it. On top of it were about a dozen folded belts. Most of them were yellow. There were a few other colors, too. But what was scary was the three chairs behind the table.

I imagined the test being like a normal class. I didn't think it would be so formal. Or have *three* judges.

At exactly ten o'clock Master Kim and two other black belts came in and walked in front of the table.

"Good luck," Madison whispered in my ear. "Don't be nervous, be awesome."

"Thanks," I said, "Good luck to you, too."

"Students," Master Kim called, "*Charyut!*"

I stood at attention like everyone else. After Master Kim called roll, he lined us up by belt color. For a change, the white belts were in the front. This didn't help my nervous stomach. Next he introduced the two guest judges. One was his father, and the other one was his brother. That only made me more nervous. Three masters in one place!

Master Kim bowed us in and wished us luck. Then he and the other judges sat down behind the table. The room went quiet, and my legs went to jelly.

We warmed up with jumping jacks. Landing on both feet at the same time made my tailbone hurt. I tried landing one foot at a time and kicking the other foot out, and that helped. I hoped Master Kim wouldn't notice I was doing the jumping jacks a different way from everyone else.

We ran through our punches, kicks, and blocks. First, Master Kim called them out in Korean. Then we repeated the command and did it. Lower block, face block, middle block, knife hand strike, front kick, roundhouse, side kick, push kick. Once I got moving, I was too busy trying to remember everything to think about the pain in my behind. Or to worry about Mom and Dad watching. I wasn't too busy, though, to forget that I was being watched by Master Kim and two other master black belts.

OW!

Master Kim got up from behind the table and picked up a kicking shield. He went down the line, giving each student a command in Korean. Even though we had just gone through all of the basic motions, my brain started flipping through channels. And all I could land on was a signal from the Emergency Broadcasting System.

I was the fourth person. When Master Kim got to me, he said, "*Yup chagi.*"

"*Yup chagi,*" I repeated.

Relax. You can do this. I mentally went through my flash cards.

Oh, right. *Yup chagi* was a side kick.

I got in my ready stance, pivoted on my front foot, brought my back leg up and around, and shot my heel out and—"*Hee-yah-owww!*"

There was a sharp pain in my tailbone. Up until then, we'd been kicking in the air. But kicking the shield was different. I returned to ready position—carefully.

Master Kim leaned in closer. "Are you all right, Eliza?"

I blinked my eyes quickly to keep the tears in check. "Yes sir."

Master Kim gave me a quick nod and went to the next student.

I sucked in my breath. *Don't cry. Don't cry. Just give it a minute.* And I was right. After a minute or two, the pain faded to a dull ache.

After everyone had a chance to kick the shield, it was time for *poomsae* or forms. The white belts started things off with *kicho il bo*. I discovered that as long as I wasn't moving too quickly, the pain wasn't bad. I wondered how my board break would go, though. I would have to snap my kick then. And it would be up against wood, not air.

I leaned against the wall while the other color belts sat down to watch the higher ranks do their forms. As usual, Madison's form was perfect. I couldn't believe Cookie was missing it.

Master Kim paired us up. Since Rosa and I were both white belts, we were partners. We faced each other and bowed. She looked as nervous as I felt. When Master Kim had his back turned, I stuck out my tongue at her to try to lighten things up. It worked. Rosa giggled.

"Everyone on this side," Master Kim said, motioning to my side of the room. "Please grab your partner's wrist."

I stepped forward and grabbed Rosa's right wrist with my right hand. With a swift pull and sharp, "Hiiii!" she escaped. We were supposed to do it several times while Master Kim wandered up and down the line, watching. Each time I grabbed, Rosa escaped, no problem. I couldn't help but feel a little jealous. I'd never been able to get mine right on the first try.

When Master Kim announced it was time to switch

roles, my palms started to sweat. Too bad my wrist wasn't sweaty. That would make escaping much easier.

Rosa reached for my outstretched wrist. I felt her fingers just beginning to wrap around my arm.

Suddenly my brain went into high gear. *Now!*

I closed my eyes, spread my fingers, yanked my arm down and out. "Hup!"

When I dared to look, I was standing a couple of feet away from Rosa. And my hands were up in a guard—both of them free and ready to fight.

I'd done it! I'd escaped first try. The trick all along was to move fast. And, shoot, I was good at moving fast.

Rosa grabbed my wrist a few more times. And when Master Kim came over to watch, I showed him a perfect wrist escape.

"Good job," Rosa whispered when it was time to shake hands.

"Thanks. You too," I told her.

DON'T BE NERVOUS, BE AWESOME

It was time for the memorization part of the test. The students stood at attention, waiting to be called up to the table. There one of the black belts would quiz you. They could ask you as many questions as they wanted. Some students came back after a short time. Others stayed for a long time. That jittery feeling came back.

Master Kim's father waved me over.

"Hello, Eliza," he said. "Please tell me the definition of taekwondo."

Yay! An easy one.

"Yes sir," I said. "Taekwondo is the art of hand and foot fighting. *Tae* means using your foot. *Kwon* means using your hand. *Do* means the art or way of life."

"Where is taekwondo from?"

Ha! Another easy one.

"South Korea," I answered.

"Good," he said. "What does *charyut* mean?"

Applesauce. I couldn't remember. It sounded familiar . . .

The judge waited with a blank look on his face. And the longer he waited, the worse it got.

"You do this every class," he prompted.

I bit my bottom lip.

"*Charyut!*" the judge said.

Without thinking, I stood at attention. Oh yeah! I felt a little silly for forgetting it for a second.

The judge smiled. "*Kamsahhamida.* Thank you. You may return to your place in line."

"Yes sir."

On my way back, Mom caught my eye and raised her eyebrows as if to ask, "Well?"

I gave her quick thumbs-up. *I can do this.*

I CAN'T DO THIS

The room buzzed when Flying Ninja Girl and the other teenage black belts helping with the test rolled out a cart of stacked boards.

Board breaks already? I felt hot and panicky, like I was going to throw up, but I couldn't tell if that was because I was excited or scared.

The color belts went before the white belts. And each color had a different board break. The orange belts were first. They had to do ax kicks. Madison was great. Her leg arched high, and then she snapped her heel straight through the board. One of the other orange belt's heels hit the board and bounced right off. He fell on his butt. He turned pink even though no one laughed.

Some of the kids broke their board on their first try. Some needed a few tries. One poor yellow belt tried and tried.

Master Kim crouched into position and held the board out in front of her.

She was doing a side kick, and it looked like she was strong enough. But her heel kept stopping the second she hit the board.

"Follow through," Master Kim told her after her third attempt.

The girl tried again. Her leg stretched out, and her heel hit the board. And stopped.

She needs to try to kick Master Kim, not just the board, I thought.

Holy lightbulb! I could finally *see* it! What Master Kim was talking about when he said to follow through.

Kicking *at* the board only got you to the board. But the board wasn't the destination. It was just a stop along the way.

"This is your final chance," Master Kim told the yellow belt. And then he got into position with the board.

"Come on," another student called out. "You can do it!" The rest of us joined in with encouraging words and clapping.

The girl got ready, took a deep breath, and tried again. Her foot hit the board right in the middle and bounced back.

Master Kim straightened up. Then he bowed to the girl and handed her the unbroken board.

"Take your seat," Master Kim told her.

The girl looked like she was going to burst into tears.

I leaned over to the boy next to me. "Does that mean she failed?" I whispered.

"She'll get another chance later," he whispered back.

Later? Later when? I wondered. I was about to ask the boy, but then I heard my name.

"Eliza," Master Kim said. "It's your turn."

"Yes sir!"

That hot and panicky feeling came back as I walked across the room to where Master Kim was holding out my board.

The only thing standing between me and my yellow belt was a half-inch-thick pine board.

Everyone in the room was watching, waiting.

And I was thinking, *I can't do this.*

I slowly practiced my push kick against the board, making sure my foot was going to land in the right place and measuring my distance. I repositioned the board one more time, nudging it just a little lower.

"Come on, Eliza," Madison called out. "You got this."

Others joined in. "Yeah. Piece of cake!"

The cheering helped.

Kicking the shield had hurt. I knew throwing my push kick against a board was going to hurt, too. Testing was starting to catch up with me. My tailbone was throbbing. This wasn't my last chance. This was my *only* chance.

I stared at the board. It stared back. *You can't do this*, it said.

And then from somewhere deep inside me, Superhero Eliza spoke up. *Oh yeah? Watch this.*

rack!

THE PART WHERE I GOT A NEW BELT

Congratulations," Master Kim said to the students. "Please turn around and remove your belts."

I set down my board—now in two pieces—at my feet. (I could still smell the pine.) And then I turned away and unknotted my belt. Following Madison's lead, I placed my white belt around my neck and turned back toward Master Kim.

I was sweaty, tired, and my butt hurt. But I couldn't stop smiling.

Master Kim explained to the audience that it was a tradition for a black belt to tie on a new belt when it was earned. Then he began handing out belts. It seemed like it took both forever and no time at all for him to get to me.

I watched as Master Kim walked to the table and picked up a yellow belt. *My* yellow belt.

He strolled over and stood in front of me. I raised my arms, and Master Kim wrapped the belt around my waist and expertly knotted it. "It is a little stiff," he said. "But you can break it in."

"Yes sir," I agreed.

Master Kim stepped back and extended his hand. "Congratulations."

"Thank you, sir."

As Master Kim walked away, I couldn't resist taking a quick look. Yellow was definitely a good color for me.

ONE MORE THING

There was a round of applause from the parents and judges as we all stood in our new belts. And then Master Kim asked the students to please take a seat for a moment. I sat down as carefully as I could.

"As my returning students know," he said, "I occasionally award special patches after a test. These patches are reserved for students who show outstanding excellence in their techniques or demonstrate true martial-arts spirit. Today I would like to honor one of our students here."

Master Kim picked up a small patch from the table and held it in his hand.

"This student did well today. It was clear she was prepared. And this was especially impressive because last week I received a phone call from this student's father telling me she had been injured and probably wouldn't be able to test."

My heart jumped a beat, and I felt my cheeks get warm. I glanced at Dad, but he was paying attention to Master Kim.

"I did not expect to see this student this morning," Master Kim went on. "I know she was still in pain, but she came anyway and performed to the best of her ability. She showed the heart and determination of a martial artist and for that, I'd like to give this Spirit Award patch to Eliza Bing."

I got to my feet slowly and walked to the front of the room. Master Kim bowed and held out the patch.

I'd never won anything in my whole life. And if I was being called to the front of the room by a teacher, it was usually because I'd done something disruptive.

I returned the bow. "Thank you, sir."

And then everyone started clapping again.

For me.

A GOOD MARTIAL ARTIST

After the test was over, everyone was talking and taking pictures.

"Congratulations," Madison said.

"You too," I said, pointing to her green belt.

"Can I see it?" she asked.

I held out the patch, which was a small white rectangle with a red border and the words SPIRIT AWARD embroidered in the middle.

"That's so cool," Madison said. "I'm jealous. He almost never gives patches to white belts."

"But I'm a yellow belt now," I reminded her.

She laughed. "Oh yeah."

Our parents walked up. Madison's dad spoke first. "Well done, ladies!"

"Yes, congratulations," Mom added.

Dad wrapped an arm around my shoulder. "I'm so proud of you."

Madison introduced her father and then announced that she was hungry. Her dad offered to take her out to eat to celebrate.

"Can we go out to eat to celebrate, too?" I asked Mom.

"Sure. Why not? You must be starving, too, after all that work," she said.

"Well, bye," Madison said to me. "Maybe I'll see you around."

"Okay, see ya," I told her.

I hated taking off my new yellow belt, but I had to change before going to lunch. I folded it carefully and put it on top of my *dobok* inside my gym bag. Mom and Dad were waiting outside of the bathroom for me.

At the restaurant, I got two orders of chicken nuggets and a large pop. (Mom found a booth with padded seats for me.) Mom, Dad, and I talked about the test and where I should I hang up my broken board.

As I was finishing off the last of my fries and ketchup, Mom pulled a yellow envelope out of her purse.

"Here," she said. "This is for you."

Inside, there was a congratulations card. On the outside was a Mr. Potato Head and the inside said, Way to go, I-da-ho!

There was also a gift card to the local mall. For fifty dollars!

I looked up at Mom in shock.

She shrugged. "I have some overtime coming to me. Once your tailbone has completely healed, I'll take the whole day off. I thought we could go shopping. Just us girls. No cell phones this time."

"You don't have to do that," I told her.

"Yes," Mom said. "I do. And besides, I *want* to."

I blinked back the tears that came without warning.

"Got any ideas of what you'd like to buy?" Dad asked.

The kicking shield I'd made out of Sam's old quilt and duct tape popped into my mind. I thought about what it would be like to have a real one. I bet we could find a used one on the internet.

"A few," I said.

Mom raised her eyebrows. "Really? Do they involve a certain cake-decorating kit for a certain fall class?"

"Well, maybe I could save some of the money for that," I said. "I think I should just keep practicing at home for a while, though."

"But I thought you wanted to be a cake decorator," Mom said.

"I do. And I'm going to be," I told her. "In fact, could we

stop on the way home and get some ingredients? I have this great idea for a cake in the shape of a broken board."

"Of course!" Dad said.

"What made you change your mind about the class?" Mom asked before she took a sip of her drink.

"I just wanna stick with taekwondo, too, if that's okay."

Mom coughed and sputtered. "Went down the wrong way," she squeaked, waving her cup.

Dad handed her a napkin, then turned to me and grinned. "I think we could probably work something out."

"Cool," I said. "Because a good martial artist never quits."

In case you get confused or just want to know how to pronounce the taekwondo words in this book, here they are.

Your friend,
Eliza (yellow belt)

ahnjoe (ahn-JOE): sit down

annyeon hashimnikka (ahn-young hahs-im-nee-ka): formal hello

ap chagi (OP cha-gee; the G is hard, like the word *go*): front kick

charyut (cha-RYUT): attention

cheonman-eyo (CHON-ma-nae-yo): you're welcome

choonbi (chun-BEE): ready position

dan (don): black belt

dee (DEE): belt

dobok (doe-BOK): uniform

dojang (doe-JAHNG): training hall. It means "House of Discipline."

hae sahn (hay SAHN): dismissed

jong yul (jong-YUL): line up

juchum-seogi jireugi (CHU-shum so-GEE ja-ROO-gee; the G is hard like the word *go*): riding-horse stance with a punch

kamsahhamida (gam-sah-hahm-mee-da): thank you very much

kicho il bo (ki-CHEW ill boo): basic form number one. *Il* means first.

kihap (KEE-hahp): yell

koomahn (khoo-MAHN): stop

kyoonyae (kyoon-YEY): bow

mushin (moo-SHIN): having no mind. Mushin is not a Korean word; it's Japanese.

poom (POOM): junior black belt

poomsae (poom-SAY): form

sabumnim (SAH-bahm-nim): master instructor

shijak (shee-JAHK): begin

taeguk il jang (Tae-GUK ill JAHNG): form representing the great principle of Heaven

taekwondo (tie-KWON-doe): the South Korean art of hand and foot fighting. *Tae* means to use the foot. *Kwon* means to use the hand. *Do* means art or way of life.

whojin (who-JIN): slide back

yup chagi (YUP cha-GEE: the G is hard, like the word *go*)**:** side kick

yursit (yur-SIT): stand up

How to count to ten in Korean

hana (HAH-na): one

dool (DOOL): two

set (SET): three

net (NET): four

dasut (DAS-it): five

yasut (YAS-it): six

ilgop (ill-GOP): seven

yuldol (yul-DOL): eight

ahop (AH-hop): nine

yul (YOOL): ten

In traditional taekwondo, you have to be fifteen years old to become a black belt, also called a *dan*. Anyone younger than fifteen is called a junior black belt, or *poom*.

Some people think having a black belt is the highest

rank you can reach, and once you get it, you're an expert. But that's not true. A black belt is just a new beginning. There are different levels, or degrees, of black belt. Each school has its own rules about testing, but in general, it takes three to five years of studying and training to become a black belt. In order to be called a "master" in taekwondo, you have to be a fourth degree black belt. Very few people who do taekwondo stick with it long enough to reach this rank or higher.